I0747999

ERASED FROM EXISTENCE

ANITHA KRISHNAN

DREAM PEDLAR PUBLICATIONS

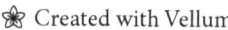 Created with Vellum

ABOUT THIS BOOK

Erased from Existence

A lavender farm in summer. A fifteen-year-old girl who loves the colours of sunset. A handsome stranger who begs her to run away with him.

It could have been a love story. Except, it is not that kind of a story.

When a strange man approaches Rebecca Classion outside her farmhouse in the dead of the night and begs her to not go back inside, she does what any sensible fifteen-year-old would do. She runs straight back into the safety of home and slams the door shut behind her.

Only, it turns out to be the worst decision of her life.

From that day on, Rebecca Classion fades away. From the memories of all who once knew and loved her. From the perception of everyone she encounters.

Not a trace of her persists for more than a fleeting instant. Not her voice. Not a footprint.

All she yearns for is to exist again in the world of her loved ones.

But oblivion may be the only safe place. After all, to be seen is to be exposed. And some truths are better left hidden.

For Abhinav & Dhruv,
truly miraculous beings who put up with my frequent
disappearances from reality without complaint

CHAPTER I

AT FIRST SIGHT

The first time I saw Marcus Ahlgren, he came stumbling out of the woods behind our farmhouse. He was moments away from death and looking for a way towards life.

It was the day I had promised to take the twins to watch the sunset. A phenomenon of astounding beauty I had discovered only the day before.

It was summer, and the days didn't seem to want to end. The sun tended to stay high up in the western sky way past bedtime for the little ones.

I had turned fifteen the week before, so Mom cut me some slack. A whole lot of slack. But my siblings, ten-year-old twins, still had strict bedtimes to follow.

So the day before I first saw Marcus Ahlgren, I strayed outside by myself, after tucking the little ones in bed, while the grown-ups retreated to the game room for yet another round of drinks and to catch up on family gossip. I knew they'd all sleep in the next morning and wake up close to lunchtime, hung-over, and perhaps a trifle embarrassed if they happened to remember how much they had let their tongues wag the previous night.

As for me, I loved the summer song of the cicadas and the vast expanse of the sky above our sweet-smelling lavender fields.

I spread out a picnic mat in the middle of the field and laid down on it. The air was thick with the sweet fragrance of the blooms.

The blue sky above me faded into a pale colourlessness, while all the colours that usually didn't belong to the skies— red, orange, purple, gold, pink—gathered on the horizon, chasing after the departing sun.

And then the first star winked at me. And then another. And the sky turned cerulean and indigo and eventually a shade of black that should have been opaque, but the light of all the stars pierced through the night sky and made it translucent somehow. As if the night sky were merely a veil, a portal to other worlds it intended to conceal.

I would have stayed there all night, not sleeping a wink, simply staring at the sky, as if I could have gouged a hole through it with my unrelenting gaze and uncovered the mysteries that lay beyond. But Mom eventually came out and asked me to come back into the house.

The next morning, I regaled Zelda and Sara with beautiful imageries of all that I had witnessed in the skies. Small black-grey clouds lined with bright purple. Planes that gleamed as they drew streaks of orange and pink contrails that puffed out like confetti in their wake.

"I want to see it too," Zelda, the more boisterous of my twin sisters, shouted at the breakfast table.

"Me too," Sara piped up. Where Zelda went, Sara followed.

"Okay, okay," I yielded. "But only after you finish your breakfast, and after we get through all our chores for the day, and after we've had a hearty dinner."

Zelda whooped with delight. Sara did too, though no matter how loud she shouted, it was almost always a whisper that drowned in the avalanche of her sister's presence.

I don't think either of them noticed it, but sometimes it was the only thing I noticed and worried about whenever I watched over my sisters.

The idea of Sara trailing in Zelda's shadow troubled me. They were born seven minutes apart, Zelda coming out shrieking and screaming while Sara had let out mere whimpers. As if even in the womb, they had known their respective places and were determined to uphold their roles in the outside world too.

Even though they were identical twins, Zelda shone like the sun while Sara twinkled like a very distant star. Too far away. Not wanting to draw attention to herself. Even Zelda's green eyes and golden hair were somehow more lustrous, more full of life, than Sara's.

Mom observed these things too, obviously, and she tried hard to encourage Sara to be more independent, become more of her own person, as subtly as she could, without drawing anyone's attention to the sibling dynamics in our home.

My heart always went out to Sara, but that was just me, attracted to the underdog, the one that rarely strayed into the limelight.

And even though Zelda never seemed aware of her own confidence, her innate ability to outshine her sister, even if only inadvertently, I couldn't help but resent her in some small measure for being a bit too much. A bit too loud. A bit too beautiful. A bit too sure of herself. A bit too full of love for this life.

So when she jumped up that morning at breakfast, as I had known she would, and declared that she wanted to watch the sun go down, I had only been too eager to make her work hard at the gift shop that day. A small price to be paid for the reward of staying up way past bedtime and soaking up the sights and sounds of a glorious summer day drawing to a close.

But whatever delight I may have secretly hoped to glean by putting Zelda in this predicament was quickly replaced by shame.

"Let her be," Mom whispered to me after breakfast as I herded the twins out of the door towards the gift shop.

Mom, sweet Mom, was all for letting her children express themselves the way they pleased. She never told us to be quiet or to go away to another room or to not make a mess. Everything we did or said was an endless source of delight to her. She basked in our very presence. Her eyes lit up whenever any of us barrelled into her orbit.

The only trouble was that she thought the world would be just as accommodating towards us, just as accepting of us, as she was. I was slowly discovering otherwise, but I couldn't bear to tell her so.

The way people looked at Zelda and held their breath, hoping she would notice them too, sprinkle a little of her shine on them, brighten up their world a little bit, share with them some of the magic she always seemed to be carrying with her, within her.

The way Sara looked up at her older sister with so much

adoration. I wondered what went on in that little child's head. Would that adoration morph into something else as the years passed? Envy? Resentment, perhaps?

"Right now, everything is perfect." Mom's voice nudged me out of my reverie.

The twins were already halfway across the lavender field, drifting and bumbling like milkweed seeds, playing a game of tag with each other as they went.

Zelda ran fast, her eyes on the destination. Sara tended to drift, stopping to smell a flower here or caress another one there, until Zelda came back and tagged her, and the game began all over again. I shook my head and chased after them, trying to soak up some of their innocence and unbridled laughter.

The gift shop stood at the entrance to the farm. It was in a large building that had once been a barn when my ancestors, the Classions, had reared horses and cattle on the farm. That was aeons before any of us were born.

Now, the barn looked like it originally did from the outside. A lick of paint had given it a new lease of life. It stood like a reminder of ancient times, the past rejuvenated and invoked into existence once again. A bright red with white trim, it drew the attention of visitors to the farm, inviting and welcoming them to step out of the present moment into a forgotten time in history.

Inside, it was so large and wide that the twins and I often played hide-and-seek on slow days. Rows and rows of in-house lavender products were stocked on neat shelves that didn't rise above my shoulders but were tall enough for the twins to hide behind without crouching.

But more often, Sara and I lost ourselves in the fantasies

that were on sale, abandoning the game altogether, much to the consternation of Zelda who, on such occasions, found herself in the role of a seeker with no one to look for.

Lavender creams and sprays to make your body and your home smell like our farm.

Aromatic sachets you could tuck in your closets for a whiff of lavender as you went about your day. Or under your pillow to give you sweet lavender dreams.

Bags of lavender tea that promised to take away all your worries.

Soaps and essential oils and body lotions to transform the fragrance of your soul.

Lavender-coloured jewellery and sculptures made by local artists.

Even a sun hat with a lavender silk ribbon that went around it and ended in a bow with a flourish.

But that morning turned out to be a busy one. No time for games and daydreams. The season had only just begun but the morning was already bustling, filled with visitors to the farm and the gift shop. Summer interns helped at the shop and on the farm, while Dad stayed in the background, checking inventory, drawing up task lists to be executed, and monitoring the interns without making them conscious of it. We tried to help and stay out of their way at the same time.

Zelda stood behind the cashier's counter, which faced the main entrance to the shop. All visitors had to enter the shop and make their way through it to the farm. Hers was the first friendly face every visitor to the farm greeted. She stood there all day, smiling sweetly at everyone who entered, greeting them heartily, inquiring about them and their interests, and giving them little tips and suggestions on how best to enjoy their time at the farm.

None of it was based on pretence. She loved our farm and our life so much that she couldn't help but share its magic with everyone she encountered.

It was great for business; I'd be the first to admit. Everyone inevitably purchased something on their way out, charmed by this little fairy, eager to remain in her good books. Zelda would have loved them even if they hadn't parted with their money. But they didn't need to know that, of course.

It was four in the evening when we three left the barn, leaving Dad and the summer interns to attend to the remaining few visitors, clean up the shop, and finally close it at the end of yet another prosperous day.

The twins and I ran to the stream that gurgled behind our home, changed into swimwear, and splashed about in the cool water like fish returning home after an impossibly long time away from it.

That was when we saw him.

CHAPTER 2
DEAD MAN'S EYES

I was the first to see Marcus Ahlgren the day he tottered into our lives for the first time. Of course, I didn't know him as Marcus right away. He was only a stranger and that's what he remained until I learnt my lesson.

That afternoon, he came from the woods further up, stumbling on a trail that ran beside the stream. He clutched his stomach and lurched from tree to tree, unable to walk more than a few steps without the aid of something to lean against. At first, I thought he was drunk.

I couldn't see his face from where we were, but his outfit was remarkable. He was dressed for riding. Breeches and high riding boots. A tailcoat too, although at the time I didn't know what it was called. It did look like a coat with a split tail at the back, so later when I learnt the name, its appropriateness was one of the few things that made sense to me, and I sometimes clung to the word like a lifeline when the world around me spun out of control.

And then there was that hat. That very cowboy hat. Widebrimmed. Casting his face in eternal shadow.

Even now when I think back to the first time I saw him, it is not his face but his outfit that comes to mind. He looked right at home emerging from those woods, traipsing through the farm, and appeared to be making his way towards our home or as close to it as he could get in his drunken, staggering gait.

"Who's that?" Zelda's high-pitched voice of excitement rang out from somewhere behind me. Everything was an adventure to her. Even the sight of a stranger. Someone new. Someone unfamiliar. A new adventure waiting to unfold. A new tale bursting to be told.

"Shh!" I tried to quell her without turning back, but it was too late. The man had already noticed us. His gaze had turned our way, drawn by her voice. I hoped he wouldn't see the twins and I tried to shield them behind me.

He raised an arm as if in greeting, but winced and promptly brought his hand back down to his side. Something was not right. He hurried towards the front entrance to our home.

I gathered the twins and our clothes, and we ran home, dripping wet and wrapped in towels. It never occurred to me to run the other way. Far, far away from the stranger.

We entered through the kitchen at the back of the house, the twins giggling as they tried not to slip on the linoleum floor. Either they hadn't sensed my alarm, or they reckoned that a stranger in our home replete with so many adults need not be feared.

A pot of pasta gurgled on the stovetop, unattended. Whoever was cooking, was not in sight. Not in the kitchen at least. I switched off the stove. Zelda and Sara dashed to the staircase in the landing that unfurled from the kitchen and raced upstairs.

I was about to follow them when I heard whispers and sobs from further down. I tiptoed across the hallway and peeped into the living room, which seemed to be the likeliest source of those muffled sounds.

Everybody was there. Mom and Dad. Grandma and Grandpa. Dad's parents, that is. Mom's family lived on another continent, the expanse of several oceans creating a wide gulf between our homes and our lives.

Uncle Jensen—Dad's brother and my favourite uncle—and his wife, Aunt Melissa. They were childless. Child-free was their choice of word. But they doted on us as if we were their very own children. Instead of looking at us as reminders of their own lack, they had simply chosen to revel in the gift we three sisters had become to them.

The grown-ups had crowded around a large, coral-coloured couch that graced the living room. Only Grandpa sat in his wheelchair nearby, fast asleep and oblivious to the commotion erupting right beside him. The wheelchair had become his most steadfast companion ever since he suffered an unexpected stroke several years ago.

Grandma huffed away from the group suddenly and that's when I saw what the grown-ups had cocooned all this while.

The man from the woods.

He lay on the couch. His eyes stared at someplace far above me, unseeing. His hat had fallen to the floor. A cry wanted to burst out of my mouth, but I put my hand in it and bit down hard. His hands lay by his side, blood-soaked, and from his abdomen protruded the hilt of a dagger.

For a moment, time stood still. As my heart skittered to a

temporary hiatus, my legs found the sense to carry me away from the living room and up the stairs and into the bathroom where the twins were soaking in a warm tub.

It wasn't until I reached the sink that I removed my hand from my mouth and finally allowed myself to heave into the basin. Violently. Noisily.

The last thing I remembered before my legs buckled and I fainted was the way the dead man's eyes had moved and settled upon mine.

CHAPTER 3
FEVER DREAM

My family believed that words have power. If you kept talking about something, that alone was an invitation for it to manifest, Mom often said to us. In these times, she'd have been accused of forcing toxic positivity down our throats.

Conversely, my family also believed that if you didn't talk about something, if you pretended it didn't exist, it would go away of its own accord. We were masters of denial too.

So when I asked Mom about the stranger on our couch, she cocked her head and touched my forehead to check for fever. I had just come to and found myself in my own room, the heavy curtains drawn, although the sun was still roaming the skies outside, which I could tell from the way the curtain was backlit faintly.

"Oh, the twins and I were going to watch the sunset," I said, suddenly remembering how the day had begun, how it had unfolded, and how we had planned to celebrate its ending.

Mom smiled at me and said, "They're already fast asleep. You all have had a busy day."

"Who was that guy, Mom?" I asked again. My voice sounded feeble to my own ears.

Mom ran her fingers through my hair, then cupped my cheeks and said, "There's no guy here, sweetie. It's just us."

The conviction with which she spoke was so emphatic that I accepted her words without question. I believed her because I wanted to. Because the alternative was simply incomprehensible.

It had been a long day indeed. Perhaps the stream had been a tad too cold, or we had spent too long splashing about in the water. Or perhaps I had caught a bug. My body shivered a little, as if confirming my hypothesis.

I turned to my side and held on to my mother's hand, still pressed against my cheek, and closed my eyes, my mind filled with the image of her. Beautiful. Serene. Nothing ever went wrong when she was around. Right then, everything was perfect.

CHAPTER 4

POPSICLE SUNSET, THEN A STRANGE REQUEST

I t wasn't until two days later that I felt strong enough to take the twins out on a sunset adventure.

It had been an unusually hot day and we had spent most of it indoors. Mom took the twins out to the stream in the afternoon, but I was reluctant to go. I pleaded weakness, but the truth was I didn't want to slip back into thinking about the illusory man who had emerged from the woods the day I fell ill. I opted for a nap, which was just as well, because I was well-rested and alert by the time evening was upon us.

We ran out with a picnic mat and a cooler stocked with popsicles. Zelda's and Sara's eyelids drooped heavily with sleep, but being outside under the vast, vast sky woke them up.

Orange and pink and purple and red. Coral and carmine and magenta. Like a child's tongue stained with the colours of too many candies eaten all at once.

For once, speech deserted Zelda. She stood gaping at the western horizon, not even blinking for fear of missing the slightest shift in the world around us. She wouldn't brook even that momentary interruption to the scene that unfolded in front of her.

I quietly placed the cooler on the ground, laid out the mat, and settled down on it. Like a girl possessed, Zelda sank onto the mat and leaned against me, still refusing to take her eyes off the horizon. Sara, too, sat down on the other side and put her small arms around my waist.

I hugged my sisters tightly and we all watched the orange sun as it disappeared, slowly but also swiftly at the same time. Darkness crept into the skies and all around us, revealing stars and fireflies that sunlight had concealed all day. Like secrets that could be safely revealed only in the shadows cast by moonlight.

The darkness of sleep must have overpowered us, for the next thing I felt was a gentle shake of my shoulder.

Even before I could open my eyes, I sensed a hollowing out on either side of me, as something or someone peeled my sisters away from me. Exposed, without the warm cocoon their small bodies had formed around me, I jolted up and rubbed my eyes so I could see.

They were only silhouettes, blacker than the night surrounding us, but it appeared to be Dad and Uncle Jensen carrying Zelda and Sara towards the farmhouse. Too groggy to jump to my feet, I followed them by sight until they opened the front door and disappeared inside. The door swung shut behind them.

That my sisters were taken back home came as a relief to me. That I was left behind, all alone, confused me. Of course, someone—Dad or Uncle Jensen—had woken me up with a shake of my shoulder. I was too old, too heavy, for either of them to carry sleepy-little-me back home. Only a boyfriend or a husband would have the privilege of carrying me henceforth, I reckoned. And I had neither. I had to rely on my own legs to shepherd myself homewards.

I rubbed my eyes and looked around. The night was aglow with the delicate light of fireflies, as if the sky had descended upon our farm and let loose her stars on the rows and rows of lavender plants.

There was something to be said about living in the countryside with bugs and solitude for company. There was plenty of both, that evening. There was nothing you could do about the bugs. And, if you were anything like Sara or me, there was nothing you needed to do about the solitude.

I was wide awake now, and even though the creatures of the night were putting on a grand spectacle, I preferred the cool softness of my bed to the bumpy ruggedness of the field under the picnic mat. Gathering up the mat and the cooler, now empty, I made my way back home.

And there he was.

A silhouette backlit by the porch light.

He sat on the topmost porch step, arms resting on knees, leaning forward a little. Either he was waiting for someone or was preparing to get up and flee.

I broke into a run. He was only a few feet away, but I wanted to make sure I reached him before he could disappear once more and leave me in doubt of his existence and my sanity. I need not have worried. He stayed put. Clearly, he had been waiting. For me.

"Who are you?" I asked, a little out of breath not so much from my brief, brisk run as from the way my nerves were rankled.

He looked at me for a long moment, not moving, not even

blinking. Only the sound and flow of my breath disturbed the warm summer air between us.

He was still dressed in his riding attire. The same garb he had donned when he had come blundering through the woods only to die on our couch.

"Didn't you die?" I croaked.

My question elicited the minutest of responses from him. He merely raised an eyebrow.

"Don't go in," he said at last. It was a command. Not a request.

"What do you mean?" I asked, wondering for a moment if I had imagined those words. But no. I had seen his lips move. He had uttered them; I was certain of that.

He continued to stare at me like a voiceless statue, and whatever shred of bravado I had been holding on to seemed to swiftly slip away.

"Please." His voice was barely a whisper when he spoke again. "Please, don't go in."

An unexpected shiver ran down my back. Dashing past him and running into the house and slamming the door behind me seemed like a great idea.

"Why not?" I asked.

But the man only gave me a long, sad look. He shrugged ever so slightly, then got up, tipped his hat to me, and started to walk away.

Wow! Seriously? This was the trouble with grown-ups. All they gave you were cryptic messages and expected you to shed whatever curiosity or common sense you may have had and follow their dictates to a tee.

"Hey, Mister!" I ran after the man and caught up with him before the night could swallow him up.

He stopped and looked back at me. Hope glimmered in his eyes as he looked from me to the house and back at me. Uh oh! I didn't want to give him false hope.

"What was all that about?" I asked. "Why shouldn't I go home?"

"Because if you do, it will be the beginning of an ending."

"The ending of what?"

"Of everything you've ever known in this lifetime of yours."

Fear held a tight grip around my throat. "Are you saying I will die?"

The man threw back his head and laughed a bitter laugh. "Death will be more merciful than what lies in wait should you walk through that door."

His words made no sense. I stepped back involuntarily, wanting to be closer to home.

The man stepped towards me, cocked his head to one side, and stretched out an arm. "Come with me," he said, "and no one else need be hurt. We could be the last ones to be consumed by this tragedy."

I froze for a moment and looked at him. He seemed earnest in his plea but there was no way to be certain. Was there ever? And what was this tragedy he kept referring to? About something coming to an end?

It occurred to me though, that were it not for the words that had spilled from his mouth and hung in the air between us, he might as well have been a lover beseeching me to elope with him in the dark of the night. The thought soothed my ruffled heart somewhat.

"You'll have to tell me more than that," I said. "I can't run away from home just because a stranger asked me to."

The man sighed and let his hand fall to his side. "I'm asking you to take a leap of faith here. Trust me? Please?"

I shook my head. And before he could say or do anything more, I hitched up my skirt as best as I could, and still gripping the cooler and the mat, I ran back home, hoping the door had not decided to lock itself on a whim at this precise moment.

Luck was on my side. I was past the threshold and inside the farmhouse in a jiffy, and I shut the door behind me without looking back to see whether the man was still there or not.

It didn't take long for sleep to overpower me, nor did any dreams assault me that night. It was the morning that held all my nightmares and unleashed them upon me, slowly but relentlessly.

CHAPTER 5
AN ALTERNATE REALITY

"We're leaving today, and you still haven't kept your promise." Zelda pouted at me from across the breakfast table. Sara sat beside her, arranging the bacon and eggs and toast on her plate exactly as her sister had.

"What are you talking about?" I asked.

"The sunset," Zelda whined.

"What about it? You were mesmerised yesterday."

"Nooo," she wailed, dragging out her irritation for as long as she could.

"What do you mean no?" I didn't understand what Zelda was going on about.

"Don't you remember?"

"Remember what?"

"You napped and you napped, and you were still napping by the time Sara and I had to go to bed," she said and pouted again.

"But that was two days ago!"

I remembered that day very well, the day I had napped

well into twilight. It was the day I had first promised to take the twins on a sunset picnic. It was the day I had taken ill after splashing about in the stream with Zelda and Sara. It was the day my sisters and I saw the stranger for the first time.

"That was two days ago," I said again to Zelda and looked at Sara for confirmation, but she too was watching her twin, the neatly arranged breakfast on her plate untouched. Like Zelda's.

"Nooo," Zelda whimpered again. "You simply wouldn't wake up from your nap yesterday."

"Hold on, Zelda," I said. Even as I spoke those words, I felt my voice falter. "Don't you remember how we took our picnic mat and a cooler filled with popsicles to the fields yesterday? Don't you remember how awestruck you were at the sight of all the colours in the sky? You both sat on either side of me, speechless." I allowed myself a small laugh here because nothing short of a miracle could ever render Zelda speechless. "It was that gorgeous."

"Mom!" Zelda whined even louder. Mom emerged from the kitchen to the dining area, bearing a plate of toast slices, but she stopped abruptly at the sight of our plates. Fully laden. Still untouched.

"What's—" Mom began but Zelda cut her short and said, "Becca is making up stories again. She says she took us to the fields at sunset yesterday."

Mom looked at me, her face crumpled with concern. "Why would you say that, honey?"

My tongue tripped over my words even as I tried to get them out urgently. "Because that's what happened, Mom," I managed to say eventually. It took quite an effort to get the words out coherently.

"Oh, honey," Mom said, putting her hand on my head and sliding it down to my cheek.

I knew that look. It was the look of compassionate denial. I had seen it earlier. The day I had asked Mom about the strange man from the woods, and she had assured me that he did not exist. Except, I had seen him last night too. Spoken with him, in fact. He had asked me to run away with him.

Good Lord! What was it he warned me of? An ending. The beginning of an ending. Well, I knew one thing that would end soon the way things were going. My sanity. At this rate my sanity wasn't likely to last much longer.

"I know how upset you must be that you couldn't take your sisters to see the sunset," Mom said, but I wasn't paying attention to her. Her words sounded distant, muffled, as if we were conversing underwater somehow.

I did, Mom. I did take them to see the sunset. And they loved it.

Those were the words that swirled round and round inside my head. I could see them clearly. Like a news ticker. Scrolling endlessly. Screaming urgency. Wanting to be seen. Wanting to be heard. Wanting to be believed.

Outside, behind where Mom stood mouthing words at me, behind where Zelda and Sara sat, their plates untouched, behind the large floor-to-ceiling glass windows that separated the outdoors from the farmhouse, a large expanse of grass met the stream on the other side.

You couldn't see the water from indoors; you had to walk almost right up to the edge to catch a glimpse of it. But you knew it was there. Gurgling and bubbling. Coming from some unknown place in the woods to the right, just beyond the lavender fields. Rushing towards and across the neighbouring farm. Like a story an author had started to write from the middle with no beginning and no ending yet.

But the skies sparkled just as blue here as everywhere else in the vicinity. The sun was just as warm and summery here. If only the sun and the sky could speak, they'd have testified to my side of the story.

"Where's Dad? Where's Uncle Jensen?" I asked, suddenly remembering that I indeed had human witnesses to back up my version of last night's events.

"Why?" Mom asked.

Pushing my chair back and getting up, I said, "They saw us last night. Out in the fields. They carried Zelda and Sara back home. Both had fallen fast asleep outside on the mat."

Mom pointed her hand upwards and said, "They're packing. We're going back to the city this afternoon. Have you forgotten?"

I had. We had come only for the weekend, but it was on Sunday that I fell ill. We had stayed back for a couple of days more to allow me time to recover. It was Wednesday now.

I ran upstairs to my parents' room and pushed open the heavy mahogany double door. Dad was stuffing his and Mom's clothes into a large suitcase set atop their enormous four-poster bed. He looked at me and shrugged helplessly, holding Mom's frilly evening gown in a little bundle in his hands as if he had rolled it up instead of folding it.

"Have you come to help me?" he asked with a sheepish grin.

"That wasn't my original plan," I admitted. "But I'm happy to help." The suitcase was full of garments crumpled up and stuffed against each other.

Dad had never been one for folding clothes, but for

reasons unknown to me he always volunteered to pack our bags whenever we set out on a trip. But he had an excellent memory and could recall precisely where a particular item was and retrieve it. I took Mom's gown from him and laid it out on the bed to smooth and fold it as best as I could.

"You're my best girl." Dad gave me a shoulder hug. He then walked towards the window and lit up a cigarette. The sweet smell of cloves and tobacco filled the room.

Of all the rooms in the farmhouse, this was my favourite. A large inbuilt closet and a chest of drawers with a wall mirror mounted above it occupied two walls of the room.

Side tables stood on both sides of the bed, but only Mom's had a reading lamp affixed to the wall above it. On Dad's side table perched a family photo taken only last year in the backyard, just behind the glass walls of the dining room where I had abandoned my breakfast only a few minutes ago.

All five of us had been trying our best to not giggle and offer only polite smiles, but we had burst into laughter when the photographer clicked the camera. Mom and Dad were looking at each other with wide smiles, enveloped in years of marital joy. I had bent over, doubling up with laughter. My hands were on my knees. But I was looking straight at the camera, and the sight of my own happy face made me smile.

Zelda's eyes were shut as if her wide grin had needed to take up all the space available to it on her face. Sara, for once, had been captured doing her own thing. With a beatific smile on her face, she was looking at a white butterfly that had flitted into the picture and was holding out an arm, as if to coax it into landing on her skin. Or as if she were releasing it into the wide, wide world outside.

"Dad," I said after a few moments, bracing myself both to pose the question and to receive his response.

He blew out a thick cloud of smoke and said, "Yes, honey?"

I hesitated. But the urge to know overpowered me. "Was it you and Uncle Jensen who carried Zelda and Sara back from the fields yesterday?"

I placed Mom's gown in the suitcase and looked at him. His forehead was creased. He was deep in thought.

"It was," he said. "Why do you ask?"

"Oh, Dad!" I sighed with relief and ran to give him a hug. He wasn't expecting me to barrel into him, but he hurriedly jerked away his cigarette-holding hand and patted my back with his free hand.

"What happened, Becca? Is everything alright?"

I stood back and told him how Zelda had accused me of bailing out on her last evening. "But I remember we three fell asleep, and you or Uncle Jensen shook me by the shoulder and woke me up. You both carried Zelda and Sara into the house, and I ... I came in right after you." I didn't see the need to recount my bizarre conversation with the stranger on the porch.

Dad looked at me and dragged deeply on his cigarette. He leaned towards the window and puffed out smoke from the corner of his mouth, not taking his eyes off me for even a second. I was so relieved I couldn't stand still. I came back to the bed and started to fix the mess he had made in the suitcase.

"Thank you, Dad, for clarifying," I said, glancing up to look at him.

He only stared at me, confused, as if I were a conundrum he was struggling to fathom.

"But it wasn't like that, honey," he said, waving his cigarette hand in the air. Wisps of smoke twisted and curled away from the burning end.

"What do you mean, Dad?" I tried to keep my voice steady, but it was too late. A sinking feeling had already taken root in the pit of my stomach and was dragging me down with it. I plonked myself down on the bed.

"*You* were not out in the fields with us," he said. "*You* were here. At home. Fast asleep."

CHAPTER 6
DENIAL AND DISAGREEMENT

My heart hammered so fast in my chest that it blurred every other sensation. Tears must have sprung into my eyes for the approaching shape of my father was nothing more than a blur, a blob. Whatever words he may have uttered were lost to the air between us, like the wisps of smoke from his cigarette. Sniffling, I could no longer discern even the clove scent of his cigarette. Everything I had once known was deserting me.

I stumbled out of my parents' room and let the door shut behind me. Tears streaming down my cheeks, I ran down the hallway towards my room at the end of the corridor, but muffled sounds, coming not from me, stopped me in my tracks. The door to another room was slightly ajar. I rubbed my eyes and cheeks, then knocked and poked my head into the room.

Aunt Melissa sat on the edge of the bed, facing the window, sobbing her heart out into a small, pink handkerchief. Uncle Jensen sat beside her, his arm around her shoulders, holding her grief as best as he could, which was not very well at all for it seemed to spill all over and fill up every nook and corner of their room.

Uncle Jensen saw me and smiled sadly. Aunt Melissa hadn't registered my presence, so I let myself in and walked around the bed so she could see me. She looked at me for a moment, as if trying to recollect who I was, or perhaps she was attempting to reconcile my incongruous presence in their room for neither the twins nor I had ever come up here. We only ever used our rooms to retire for the night and to stash away our luggage, which meant that even though we spent a lot of time with Uncle Jensen and Aunt Melissa, we never had much of a reason to come up here.

When she registered my presence, Aunt Melissa made no attempt to hide her tears. This is what I loved best about my uncle and aunt. They never saw the need to hide their emotions from the twins and me. Whereas I'd never seen my mother cry, nor had I seen my father overly concerned about his business affairs. Running a farm could hardly be stress-free work, yet he never got into a sweat in our presence.

Aunt Melissa held out a hand and put it around my waist as I sat beside her on the bed.

"What's going on?" I asked.

"I … I … don't know," Aunt Melissa said with much difficulty, sobs mangling her words. She burst into a fresh bout of tears.

"Change is really hard on her," Uncle Jensen explained. "Every time we leave from here, a great sorrow overpowers her. As if we're leaving a part of our souls behind."

He hugged his wife tighter and kissed her on the top of her head. She sank into his chest but held on to me too at the same time.

I supposed I understood what he meant. It was not merely the place but our time together. They'd miss us too, the twins and me.

I leaned into Aunt Melissa. Words appeared completely unnecessary, and I was happy to not have to say anything.

Instead, I took in their room. The walls were pastel pink, as if the room had once been painted to welcome the arrival of a baby girl.

Indeed, there was a rumour in the family that Aunt Melissa had miscarried a long time ago, and that the incident had rendered her unable to conceive any more children.

Mom and Grandma had long made it clear that no one was to broach the topic in the family ever again, and we did as we were told. That didn't stop us from thinking about it occasionally. Every time Aunt Melissa's eyes lit up at the sight of us, I wondered if she'd have loved us less had she had children of her own.

The realisation that the affection she bestowed upon us could have been whisked away by a quirk of fate often made me hug her a little tighter, listen to her a little more keenly, and help her out with errands much more than I did for Grandma or, sometimes, even Mom.

Apart from the bed we were sitting on, the room held only a large chest of drawers tucked under the window in front of us. The top of the cabinet was mostly empty barring two framed photographs. One was of Uncle and Aunt, both smiling at the photographer. Aunt Melissa had one arm in the air as if she were about to gesture something to the photographer but whatever she may have wanted to say or do was frozen in time forever.

The other was of all of us taken in the lavender fields only last year. I was all too familiar with it. Grandpa and Grandma, Uncle Jensen and Aunt Melissa, Mom and Dad, and the twins and I, all nine of us stood in two neat rows and presented joyful smiles to the photographer.

"You don't seem all that happy too, Bonnie m'dear," Aunt Melissa said when her tears had subsided. Her voice was soft but thick; the words struggled to form around the chokehold of emotions. I had been so lost in my thoughts it took me a while to register what she said.

"Bonnie?" I asked.

Aunt Melissa frowned. "Oh, I meant Becca. Sorry, my child." She hugged me tight and gave a little snort of surprise. "Never knew any Bonnie in my life. Wonder where that came from?"

"A slip of the tongue," I said. *Old age*, another voice in the back of my head whispered.

"Or maybe I meant to say honey." Aunt sighed and patted me on the shoulder. "You're such a dear. I'll miss my girls terribly."

"We'll miss you too," I whispered. For a few moments in the light of Aunt's grief, I had forgotten my own predicament. And now it seemed silly to bother Uncle and Aunt with it when they were drowning in their own sorrow. I could always ask them later.

And who knew? Maybe I had gotten it all muddled up. Maybe I had been having a nap after all. I may have dreamed it all up. Late afternoon naps tended to fill my head with the most bizarre of dreams. And truth be told, I hadn't been quite myself ever since I had fallen ill. After that splash in the stream with my sisters. When we had seen the … I didn't want to think about him anymore. That stranger from the woods.

Maybe I had conjured him too into existence through a dream or my imagination. A product of a nightmare. Yes, that was the most likely explanation.

The relief that arose from this thought was so overpowering I wanted to lie down and rest. A huge burden had been lifted from my shoulders, and I was tempted to let my body sag lower and lower and curl up and fall asleep.

"Would you like to take a nap, m'dear?" Aunt Melissa's soothing voice jerked me back into wakefulness. She ran her fingers over my scalp.

"That feels so good," I murmured. I could have fallen asleep then and there in my Aunt's arms, curled up on her lap, but she was still too distressed and I did not want to add to her burden. And so I said, "I better start packing too."

"Take your time. We don't leave until well after lunch," Uncle Jensen said.

I closed the door behind me when I left the room, and it was just as well I did that because Zelda and Sara chose that moment to come running down the hallway towards me. Mom was climbing up the stairs behind them.

"You've also been telling stories about seeing a man in the woods." Zelda wagged a finger at me accusingly.

"Zelda!" Mom's stern voice floated down the landing, but she was still a few feet away and her call was not forbidding enough to stop Zelda who was now prattling on about the promises I had made to her but failed to keep.

I turned towards Mom. "What's Zelda talking about? What did you tell her?"

Mom came huffing towards us, breathless from having dashed up the stairs after the twins and no doubt flustered by the explanation she now owed me.

"I had to ask them, Becca," Mom said. "What do you expect me to do? You tell me you saw a stranger inside our home, and you don't want me to take it seriously?"

"But you brushed it away," I shouted, "as if I had made things up."

Mom sighed. She was not one to hold difficult conversations. She liked it when everyone got along, when everything went well. Whenever something threatened to spin our lives out of orbit, she hastened to bring everything back to a familiar equilibrium, whether or not it was appropriate.

"You were delirious with fever, honey," she said at last, wringing her fingers. I looked down at her hands, which must have made her conscious of her act of nervousness, for she put one hand on her hip and the other on the wall. "I didn't want to upset you further. But I took your words seriously and made inquiries." She glanced at Zelda but looked back at me almost immediately.

"By telling Zelda and Sara what I confided in you?" I yelled.

I didn't know why I was so mad at her that morning. No doubt, frustration had been building up in me since Zelda picked a fight with me at breakfast. And not one person had been able to corroborate my version of last evening's events so far.

Still, it didn't explain why I felt such immense rage surge from somewhere deep within me and spill out, wanting to devour and devastate everything, everyone, that stood in its way.

Even as I stood there, pondering, waiting for an answer but also not wanting to hear anything Mom had to say in response, something shifted.

It was the slightest of movements.

Very subtle.

Almost invisible.

Zelda took a small, dainty step towards Mom and held her hand, all the while looking at me with large, frightened eyes.

Sara moved along with her sister, as if they were one. Two minds communicating without words. Two bodies dancing in unison. Where one went, the other followed. No questions asked. No answers given.

In that instant, it became them versus me. Or perhaps, this shift had already occurred in these past few days after I had taken ill, walking around in a world of my own that oddly didn't seem to tally with the world the others inhabited. And I was beginning to realise it only now.

All this while, it had been Mom and me. For the first five years of my life, it had been only Mom and me. And then the twins had come along. But Mom and I were still a team, a unit. I was Mom's little helper when it came to looking after the twins. She always said so.

Even if the whole world threatens to fall apart, I know I can always rely on you, Becca. And you, on me. That was what Mom always said to me.

What happened now? Somehow in the act of growing up, I seemed to have grown away from her.

I looked from Mom to Zelda. Zelda. She was the culprit. Cowering behind Mom, as if terrified of my wrath, she could fool Mom and her twin sister, but not me.

"You," I said, pointing a finger at her and taking a step forward. She sank back, along with Sara, and Mom put a protective arm around them to shield them from me.

What a laugh! The twins now needed protection from the

older sister who had helped change their diapers and taught them how to put away their toys, who had used her hard-earned money to buy them surprise treats and books, who had read to them late into the night in the light of a torch under the sheets long after Mom had turned out the lights in the room, who had watched reruns of Disney movies with them whenever one or both of them had fallen ill.

"You! Zelda!" I snarled, peering around Mom but not stepping any closer to the trio. "You saw that man in the woods that day when we were playing in the stream."

Zelda shook her head but didn't say anything.

"You saw him and screamed, *'Who's that?'*" I said, mimicking her shrill call, the one designed to draw all attention to her. "That's what made him turn around and take notice of us."

Mom turned around to look at Zelda.

"No, Mom," Zelda said, shaking her head furiously.

"Liar!" I stepped towards her, but Mom was quick to put an arm out to stop me.

"Get a hold on yourself, Becca," Mom admonished me.

"But Mom, she's lying! She saw him too," I said. Hot tears were flowing down my cheeks. "Why don't you tell the truth, Zelda?" I beseeched her once more.

"Stop shouting at her! There was no man in the woods!"

The voice was loud and unfamiliar. But it had the power to stop us in the midst of our madness. So rarely had it been used.

Mom, Zelda, and I turned to look at Sara.

For it was she who had spoken.

The younger twin.

The shy one.

The quiet one.

The meek one.

Sara too looked taken aback, as if the words had forced their way out of her mouth without her permission. For a moment, she looked larger than whiny, pouty Zelda.

Even in my anger, I couldn't help but feel a sliver of pride and awe slip-slide through my raging innards and tug the corners of my mouth into a small smile.

But then the incongruousness of the situation seemed to catch up with all of us, especially Sara. She blushed and spread out her hands and shrugged and shook her head and said, more softly now, "What? If Zelda says there was no one in the woods, then that's all we need to believe."

Then she stepped around me and walked to the twins' room. Zelda hesitated for a moment but followed her sister, and Mom went with them. I stood watching their backs until they disappeared into my sisters' room and shut the door behind them.

Standing alone in that long, endless corridor, I realised for the first time that even with all my family behind the closed doors of so many rooms, I was utterly alone.

The voices of Zelda and Sara and Mom stayed with me. The words they had spoken and the words they had left unsaid hung in this empty hallway, bouncing off the walls, ricocheting in my mind over and over again until they were all a large, overwhelmingly accusatory jumble.

I wondered if Dad or Uncle Jensen and Aunt Melissa had heard the altercation outside their rooms. And if they had, why hadn't they stepped out?

Perhaps Dad had put it down to a ladies' spat, as he often labelled disagreements between the women in the family, and refused to be dragged into it. Aunt Melissa wouldn't have wanted to come out in her grief-laden state and subject herself to unwelcome questions from Mom or the twins. Uncle Jensen would have wanted to stay by his wife's side. After all, the twins and I squabbled almost every day and made up immediately after. It was nothing out of the ordinary. A house full of young children was bound to be noisy.

Grandma and Grandpa hadn't been up to the first floor in more than a decade now ever since Grandpa had become wheelchair-bound following a stroke several years ago and Grandma had developed arthritis at around the same time.

Their rooms were on the ground floor, and they never had any reason to navigate the wide, winding stairway from which the first-floor landing unfurled on both sides, like a river forking into two.

In that moment of loneliness, I wished I had had a cousin sister of my age. If only Uncle Jensen and Aunt Melissa had not miscarried their child! The crudeness of my own thought appalled me, and I ran to my room and slid under the covers and pulled them over my head, wishing the claustrophobic darkness would somehow stop this nonstop swirl of crazy thoughts in my mind.

CHAPTER 7

LEFT BEHIND

I woke up with a start.

My heart thumped in my chest with so much force I wondered if I was having a heart attack and was about to die. Could fifteen-year-olds die of cardiac arrest? It seemed unlikely but so many weird things had happened in these past few days that nothing seemed impossible anymore.

The thought brought tears to my eyes. Hot, thick tears flowed rapidly down the side of my face and trickled around and behind my ears.

I stayed in bed, feeling pinned to it, reluctant to move until the pounding in my chest subsided.

It didn't. I waited for what seemed like a long time until lying down and waiting for the ache to pass seemed more unbearable than the squeeze in my chest itself. I pushed away the blanket and slid off the bed slowly.

My suitcase sat under the window. Ugh! I still had to pack.

But more importantly, my stomach rumbled, and my head hurt. And I didn't feel good about the spat I had had with Mom and the twins earlier that morning.

So I stepped out of my room and paused right outside the twins' bedroom door. Their room was next to mine, and we even had doors opening into a connecting chamber through the common wall that divided our rooms. I chose to knock on the main door instead, not wanting to assume their forgiveness before they had actually granted it. Especially Zelda.

My heart swelled at the thought of my sisters. They were only little children. All Zelda had wanted was to watch the sunset. I was no longer mad at her. If she couldn't remember last evening's picnic, that was all there was to it. I would have taken her today were we not due to head back to our home in the city. So I would make it up to her the next time we came here, which would in all probability be in only a fortnight from now.

With a surge of love in my heart, I knocked on their door and pushed it open.

The room was dark. The curtains were drawn, which was unusual for this time of the day.

I stepped inside and looked around.

The room was tidy. And empty.

The bunk beds had been made. A white sheet had been draped over each of the two beds, the way it was usually done to protect the linen from gathering dust.

Entering the twins' room was typically an assault on the senses. Their clothes and accessories often lay scattered on the floor, on their beds, on the couch beneath the window, atop the chest of drawers they shared. On every visible surface, in fact.

It was always an explosion of childhood. Little bits of preteen life bursting at the seams and spilling over, impossible to contain and confine to standards of tidiness and order.

But there was nothing now. No glittery hair clips to accidentally step on. No sparkly nail paint spilling from the top of the dresser onto the wooden floor beneath. No rainbow-coloured scrunchies or hairbands lay littered like wildflowers or colourful twigs anywhere. Only the faintest fragrance of their lavender bath gel lingered in the air.

"Zelda? Sara?" I called out to them, but my own voice greeted me back in response, echoes joining in my calls like a never-ending plea.

A mild panic gripped my heart. Perhaps they were playing a silly game of hide-and-seek and were about to startle me. Burst out at me out of nowhere. Well, I'd certainly deserve that after the way I had yelled at them this morning.

I'd even settle for that. Insults. Accusations. Anything other than this unresponsive silence. This indifference.

I opened the door that led to the narrow chamber connecting my bedroom to theirs. It too was empty.

I ran out to the hallway and opened the closed doors one after another. All the doors I had knocked on this morning. All the rooms I had entered this morning were empty. Shrouded in as much darkness as heavy curtains could create at mid-day. All the curtains were drawn. All the beds had been neatly made. Each room was as empty as every other.

Perhaps everyone had packed their bags and headed downstairs.

"Mom? Dad?" I shouted, as I ran down the wide, central staircase, holding on to the railing.

I ran past the living room to the guest room tucked near the entrance to the house but cleverly out of sight. That was where my grandparents stayed when they visited the farmhouse.

It too was empty. Even Grandpa's wheelchair was nowhere to be seen.

Tears stung my eyes. I ran into the living room, then into the kitchen and the dining area, calling out to everyone, desperate to see someone or hear their voice. But the Universe was determined to not grant me any wishes on this day.

I ran to the front of the house and pulled the main door open. The driveway was empty. Our midnight-blue SUV was gone. So was grandparents' vintage sedan. Uncle Jensen and Aunt Melissa's convertible was nowhere to be seen.

My body trembled with a realisation that my mind was still unable to come to grips with.

My family had simply left without me.

A strange laugh escaped my throat at the absurdity of that notion. How ridiculous! Why would they ever do something like that? Leaving me behind like an unwanted pup a family could no longer look after.

Mom and Dad loved me. They wouldn't simply go without me, would they?

Maybe they were running errands. Or perhaps there was an emergency? Grandpa? Perhaps something had happened to him, and he had to be taken to the hospital. Surely all hands were needed on deck?

I looked all around. Everything was as it had always been. The lavender plants swayed in the breeze. Their light purple colour made the blue sky look bluer. More intense somehow. The sun was almost overhead. It was noon. Lunchtime.

The winding driveway lined with tall pine and maple trees on both sides curved and met a pair of fancy black metal gates, which proudly displayed arched tops with decorative finials. It was the first and most visible part of the farm from the road. A welcome sight after the long drive from our townhouse in the city. The gates were designed to swing inwards in welcome whenever a vehicle approached them. And long before I learnt about key fobs and sensors, I used to think it was magic that made them open like that.

I started to walk down the driveway but the tingle of fallen pine needles and the sharp poke of gravel reminded me I was barefoot. It brought me to a halt, and once more tears pricked my eyes. It seemed to be the only response I had to everything going awry that day. Even the slightest pinprick was adequate to bring me to my knees. I still couldn't wrap my head around the fact that everyone was gone, leaving me and this great, rambling house and its fields behind.

It took a while but eventually fear and grief gave way to anger, and a sudden resolve blossomed from my gut and gripped me. Instead of acting like a helpless damsel in distress, I could very well make my own way home. It wasn't as if I was trapped within the confines of this property.

The instant I started to seek them, myriads of possibilities presented themselves to me. A telephone call. A hitch-hike. Buoyed up by renewed enthusiasm and determination, I turned back towards the house and—

"Aaaahh!!"

The scream that erupted from my throat was so loud and shrill that it startled a flock of ravens into unexpected, noisy flight from their treetop roosts. I screamed and screamed and maybe I wanted to or maybe I didn't want to, but either way I couldn't stop screaming, because I was terrified of what was about to come next.

For there, right in front of me, not even at arm's length,

stood the strange man. The one from the woods. The one from the night of the sunset picnic that no one else in my family had seemed to remember.

Even as I screamed myself hoarse, I couldn't bear to look at him. I squeezed my eyes shut in terror and covered my ears with my own hands and sank to the ground and curled myself up into a foetal position, wishing more than ever for the safety of a cocoon or a womb to be encased in.

Eventually I stopped screaming. But only because I ran out of voice. My body continued to tremble, fear and shock rippling through it in relentless spasms. I lay sobbing on the gravel, terrified even more now at the prospect of having to navigate this bizarre situation while defending myself from a strange man who only last night had asked me to not go back into my own home.

It was embarrassment, not anger, that eventually saw me open my eyes and sit up. The tears had dried up and I wiped my cheeks and looked around. The man was not towering over me as I had feared. He had retreated during my melt-down and was now perched on the topmost step of the patio, which is where I had seen him last night. An obstacle between me and my home.

If he saw me as weak prey, if he saw me the way I saw myself right now, nothing would stop me from becoming his victim. If only I could pull myself together, chin up, chest out, and walk like a lioness, channel all my emotions into some sort of power I could use rather than be crushed under their weight, I knew I could put up a darn good fight.

And that is what I did.

I pulled myself together, got up and walked with delib-erate steps towards the farmhouse, towards the door, towards him, not taking my eyes off him for even a moment.

"You're intruding," I said, looking down at him when I reached the patio.

He shrugged, took off his hat, and held it to his chest. "My apologies, Miss," he said.

He may have been sardonic, but I couldn't tell. He looked as sincere and serious as one could possibly look, but even someone with a poker face could convey the same impression.

He was older than I had assumed so far. Lines were etched on his forehead and around his eyes. His skin was a leathery brown, likely a consequence of too many hours in the sun, coaxing the earth to yield more and more grains to nourish the rest of the world.

But his clothes were remarkably free of blemish. His tailcoat and breeches appeared new. And so did his riding boots. Or perhaps they were well cared for. As if he worked his body to a punishing extent and in turn rewarded it by clothing it well.

"Make your way out of here and don't ever come back," I said, as sternly as I could, which was not very much so when I considered my choice of words.

So I walked backwards and climbed down the two steps I had navigated towards the front door while delivering that command, stooped a little so the man could see I was looking at him down my nose, jabbed a finger into the air in front of his face, and hissed, "Get the fuck out of here. Right. Now."

And without wasting another instant, I stormed past the front door and banged it shut behind me.

There. That felt good.

Now I understood why people swore and cursed in the

midst of a fight, verbal or physical. It gave one a sense of power, a sense of authority. When I swore at the man, I managed to diminish him somehow. He became the target of my anger, my rage. I was no longer the vulnerable one. He became the victim, though he was clearly asking for it. Turning up at the house like that. Uninvited. Unannounced. Who the hell was he?

Well, whoever he was, I didn't need a stranger lurking around the property when I was all alone in here and yet to come up with a plan to leave.

A plan. That's what I was about to come up with when I had turned back from the driveway and had almost collided with the creep.

I didn't have a mobile phone yet, Mom and Dad having stood by their promise to get me my first cell phone only on my sixteenth birthday. In the weeks leading up to my fifteenth birthday, I had held out hope that they might change their mind and surprise me with a much-needed accessory a year earlier than they had planned. But no. No such luck.

Although what they gave me far surpassed any gift they could have possibly given me ever. It was a custom-made flip-book documenting the first almost-fifteen years of my life. I went upstairs to my room and pulled it out of the topmost drawer of my dresser, just like I had done at least once every day since I had received it.

Composed entirely of photos, the first of which was taken on the day I was born and the last taken exactly a month before I turned fifteen years old, the book was as thick as an encyclopaedia but when I held it with both hands, it rested comfortably on my palms, like a very teensy newborn.

There were hundreds of photos taken in the first year of

my life alone. Mom, teary-eyed as I flipped through the pages over and over again, watching myself age nearly fifteen years in the span of a few seconds, had lamented that I had always been in a terrible rush to grow up. That I had changed every day in the first year of my life.

She didn't sound as if it were my fault, or hers for that matter, this strange way in which time stretched out days to endlessness but conversely shrunk months and years into blurry blobs that left her wondering when and how her baby, her firstborn, had grown up so much. Fifteen years gone in the blink of an eye.

I never understood her sentiment. I didn't share her longing for my babyhood. How could I long for something I had no memory of? But she said I'd know when I became a mother myself and in the same breath reminded me that there was no rush; now was the time for me to enjoy my adolescence, experience love and heartbreaks, spend endless hours on decisions over higher studies and career choices, for there'd be plenty of time to marry and have babies and forego sleep and peace of mind for good.

Mom often spoke in contradictions. Lamenting the swift passage of time one moment, only to reassure me of its abundance the very next instant.

Ah, well! I guess I needed that reassurance then. I needed all the time I could get to come up with a plan to make sense of all that was happening to me right then. I put the book back into the drawer and ran back down to the hallway on the ground floor to the landline that was hooked to the wall under the stairs and right beside the kitchen and dining area.

I dialled Mom's mobile phone first. The number, along with Dad's and our home address, had been etched into my memory since I was five years old. It rang a few times and went into voicemail. Even the twins had to learn it when they turned five. Every once in a while, Mom and Dad quizzed us on their contact details to ensure we'd even be able to recite it from our graves if asked to.

I called her a few more times, getting slightly more and more desperate with each try, and finally left a voicemail for her, asking her to come and pick me up from the farm.

Only after I had hung up did I wonder whether I ought to have mentioned the man or not. Instinct told me it would only worry her needlessly. Besides, she had already dismissed him as a figment of my imagination on more than one occasion. The memory of my last conversation with her, that spat on the landing with her and the twins, triggered yet another bout of anger and disappointment in me. And for a fleeting second, just a fleeting second, I was happy they were gone.

My hand hovered over the wall phone as I debated what to do. From where I stood, I could see the dining area and beyond, through the floor-to-ceiling windows and the yard and the stream beyond.

It was the prospect of being alone in this vast house with that strange man lurking outside that brought me to a quick decision. I picked up the receiver, called Mom's number again, and when it went to voicemail, as I had come to expect it would, I left her a message saying exactly that— that I was all alone at home and that a strange man was lurking outside, and if she cared for her firstborn, she ought to hightail it back to the farm and pick me up and take me home, our place in the city, or wherever else they had gone off to.

I called Dad's number a few times, expecting and receiving

more of the same incessant ringing and an automated request to leave a voicemail, and left a similar message for him too.

I called the landline at our home in the city and left a message there too.

And then it occurred to me to dial another number. The number I should have dialled in the first place.

911! Surely, they'd be able to rescue me from here!

With renewed hope, I called the local emergency number. An automated voice trilled cheerfully into my ear, "The number you've dialled does not exist."

This was the last straw that broke my resolve. I burst into an unexpected bout of laughter and tears at the same time until I could no longer tell whether I was laughing or crying.

For the sake of validation, I dialled 911 a few more times and got the same message, which elicited in me that strange maniacal laughter each time.

And because everything was going awry, I also dialled 999 for good measure but the same voice trilled, with an eerily British accent though, and said, "Nice try, m'dear! But this numb-ah too does not exist."

Looking back now, I think that was when I had already made up my mind about how things were to unfold thereon. If my family had abandoned me, they weren't coming back to rescue me, were they?

Because it was from this thought that the events that followed emerged. Had I not abandoned hope of being reunited with my family, I reckon I'd have pursued other avenues, other alternatives to get out of this rambling, deserted farmhouse and reunite with them in the city. But I didn't. At least, not right away.

Something had shifted in my world, and this new version

of life I found myself in seemed very intent on not letting me slip back into the older version, the one in which I had a family. To laugh with. To bicker with. To live with through all the chaos of life. Not anymore.

And it was the first time that I came close to giving up.

But then my mind conjured up the next possibility. And once again, I tried to escape.

CHAPTER 8
ALL ROADS LEAD HOME

I donned socks and running shoes. I also changed into more sensible walking attire—shorts and a T-shirt. I grabbed my knapsack and threw in it a change of clothes, sunscreen, and a towel. I went back down to the kitchen and prepared cheese and avocado sandwiches. I also grabbed a couple of oranges, two bars of chocolate, and two bottles of water, and packed them neatly into my knapsack. I checked and double-checked all the windows and doors of the house and made sure they were locked, all the while keeping an eye out for the strange man. He was nowhere to be seen.

Hat on my head, sunglasses on my face, sunscreen on my skin, and knapsack on my back, I let myself out and locked the main door of the farmhouse behind me.

Gravel crunched beneath my sneakers as I walked down the driveway. The sun hadn't moved much in the sky, it was still right overhead, so I walked in the shade of the towering pines and maples, determined to make my strength and stamina last for as long as they could.

There was a moment of hesitation when I reached the

decorative metal gates that marked the beginning or, depending on how you chose to look at it, the end of our property. I held out a key fob and pressed one of the two buttons on it. Much to my delight, the gates swung silently inwards. I didn't waste a moment questioning this unexpected stroke of good luck, and dashed out of the gates onto the road before they could swing shut.

I crossed the road to the other side for two reasons. One, so that I'd walk in the direction facing the oncoming traffic. No sidewalks flanked this rural road, which was two lanes wide but was also very smooth and bereft of the potholes and cracks that marked the pitted roads of the city.

The other reason was that I wanted to put as much distance as was possible between myself and the farmhouse. When I was packing my knapsack, I had the strangest feeling that the house would keep me trapped there for as long as forever lasted.

I still couldn't wrap my head around the sudden disappearance of my family. Every trace of their existence in the farmhouse just that morning was completely erased. As if they were the ones I had conjured out of my imagination and I had misplaced them somehow. And then there was my inability to contact them, or even the local emergency number, by the only means of communication available there.

All that pointed to some strange conspiracy of the Universe to keep me away from the rest of my family. A cosmic joke being played out at my expense. And my family's too.

I knew the way back home. First, I'd have to traverse several kilometres straight down this rural road. There was little danger of straying into side roads because, for the most part, the only divergences from the main road led to the driveways of neighbouring properties. An occasional road would intersect the main road, but so long as I kept going down this path, I'd reach the heart of the city from where home would only be a cab ride or even a bus ride away.

With hope in my heart, I set forth, not daring to give the lavender fields a second glance as I walked past them although I could see the unmistakable swathe of light purple dancing out of the corner of my eye.

Eventually, lavender gave way to the monotonous green grass and white picket fences of horse farms where the majestic animals grazed, swishing their long tails periodically.

It was a beautiful day. The sun was high in the sky but did not burn. The sky was an autumnal blue, so bright it looked substantial, made even more so by the white fleecy clouds that drifted across its face. It was only the shrill cries of cicadas and the dark green hue of tree leaves that served as a reminder of the season. Summer. Not yet autumn.

Not a single vehicle roared up or down the road in what must have been ten or fifteen minutes since I set out from home. Even bicyclists were conspicuous in their absence.

All the houses I passed were deserted. No homeowners mowing their front lawns. No visitors picking strawberries. No farmhands busy at work. It was as if this part of the world had been cleansed of human beings.

Despite the nagging sensation in the pit of my stomach that told me something was still horribly wrong, I was determined to stay the course. I kept walking and walking, reminding myself that each step brought me closer to home, praying silently to whoever was listening to lead me homewards.

And listen they did.

For in the distance, a small strip of purple appeared on the horizon. It confused me for ours was the only lavender field in this area as far as I knew. My legs moved faster of their own accord with some unspoken urgency, and I didn't take my eyes off the purple patch that looked like a bright-hued cloud keeping land and sky glued to each other.

For a long time, the tall pines and maples that lined the road revealed nothing else. But when I was close enough, nothing could conceal the attractive curlicues of the double gates and the driveway behind it that led to my farmhouse beside the lavender field.

Life had come a full circle and brought me right back to the beginning, to where I had set out from.

I stood staring at the gates like a fool, open-mouthed, when they swung open by themselves. An invitation to enter.

Whether the invitation was meant to be alluring or not, I never knew. What I remembered though was the jolt of terror that shot through my spine when realisation set in, when it dawned upon me firmly and irrevocably that I had walked away from the farmhouse only to be led straight back to it.

My body trembled like a leaf rudely shaken by particularly gusty winds. How long had I been walking for? I didn't have a watch or a phone to check, so I looked up at the sky where the sun remained pinned to that overhead spot like an eye in the centre of the world above, watching every move of mine without pausing to blink.

A strange cognisance, which felt like it didn't belong to me at the time, rose from my gut and pushed me, as if with a pair of hands, into a run. Away from the lavender fields. Away from the farmhouse. Away from the yawning chasm the open gates were, ready and willing to devour me.

Only this time I ran in the opposite direction, back the way I had come, though deep in my gut I knew this was the wrong way. This way led northwards, but the city where I lived with my family in our lavish downtown home, where I went to school and hung out in cafes and went to the movies with friends, lay firmly to the south.

Yet I ran, naively believing that the farther away from the farmhouse I went, the closer I'd somehow get to my parents and my sisters and our home in the city.

When the patch of lavender came into view again and the gates revealed themselves once more, already wide open, as if theirs was an invitation that couldn't be refused, I was not surprised. Terrified, yes. But not surprised.

And so it was with a strange calmness, the kind that comes with an attitude of surrender, and a very palpable sense of terror-laced relief that I walked past the gates and up the driveway, and I knew without turning back to look that the gates would have swung shut silently behind me of their own volition. When I reached the patio, I sat on the topmost step and waited.

My vision grew blurry with each fresh bout of tears that sprung from my eyes. My face was wet from the tears streaming down my cheeks. My hands moved up to wipe my face repeatedly. Hunger gnawed at my insides, but my mouth was too thick and my throat was too swollen and shut with fear and sadness to welcome the prospect of eating.

Yet, a tiny part of me had found a modicum of acceptance and was clinging to it as the only hope of finding a way through whatever was going on; whether it was a way *out* of it or not, there was no way to tell. As long as I held on to that tiny sliver of resoluteness, I could pretend all this was happening to someone else and not me. I could pretend everything would work itself out somehow, eventually, as long as I kept my wits about me for the time being at least.

That was the moment I ceased to exist for the rest of the world, the world of the living, the strange man told me long after.

That instant of disassociation. Of disconnection. As if it were somehow my fault. As if he were accusing me of having conjured up all that had happened to me. Turned out that blaming the victim was an age-old practice.

I have relived that moment countless times since, occasionally giving in to the temptation of ruminating, churning the incidents over and over again in my head until the story took its present form, this shape in which I have been presenting it to you. But who's to say this is what truly transpired?

This is what I remember. My memory may have unwittingly distorted the truth more than it may have intended to. A survival mechanism, you see. A way to live with the things we've done, the things that have happened to us. A way to keep ourselves from going under, crushed by the weight of our regrets and our helplessness.

Which was why when the stranger from the woods appeared from around the bend in the driveway—that curve that hid the gates from where I sat on the front porch, that camber which kept the house hidden from the eager, searching eyes of curious passers-by on the road beyond the gates—I realised at last I was ready and willing to hear what he had to say.

Besides, there was nothing else to be done.

He came with a look of defeat on his face, mouth curving downwards, eyes solemn and grave, not quite managing to conceal the effort it took him to keep his back ramrod straight and walk with purpose, not resignation.

He was dressed in his usual riding attire. Like a uniform he could not bring himself to change out of.

Despite the apparent heaviness of his garb, he trod noiselessly on the gravel. The sun was still overhead, lighting up the world in a gentle, balmy brightness that didn't hurt my eyes, but I had to blink often to soothe my weary eyes, raw and dry from having shed too many tears in a single morning.

Which was why it took me a while to notice and believe what I saw. Or rather, what I didn't see.

It wasn't until the man was right in front of me that I understood what was missing. What should have been there but wasn't. His shadow.

CHAPTER 9
A CURSE FROM ANOTHER LIFETIME

"You're not real," I whispered.

The man took his hat off his head, letting loose a mop of honey-brown curls that fell to his shoulders, and then sat down beside me.

"Neither are you," he said. "Not anymore." His voice was smooth and deep, as if the words he uttered came from somewhere deep inside of him, gathering weight and substance as they traversed up and out of him into the ether.

"What about all this then?" I waved my hand in an expansive gesture to indicate the fields to our left, the driveway unfurling from under our feet, the world beyond the gates, and the house behind us. "Are these also not real?"

"They existed for you only so long as you did. Now they are unreal to you. To me. But not to the others."

"Others?"

He nodded. "Yes. Your family."

"And yours?"

"Long dead and gone. Killed by yours."

"What!?" I whipped my head around to look at him.

"That's what all this is about," he continued matter-of-factly, looking at the empty driveway, then at the fields, and then up at the white tufts of clouds that had sneaked up and were making their way in front of the sun, casting this little patch of our world into momentary shade.

"Who killed whom?" I asked, wondering what this slip-sliding of my being into a nonsensically inexplicable situation had to do with murder.

"Family feud," he said simply. "Centuries ago."

"What does that have to do with us now?" I practically screamed in his face, more to elicit some sort of a reaction from him than to make myself heard.

Prising the story out of the man proved harder than solving a two-thousand-piece jigsaw puzzle, a feat I had managed to accomplish several times, I'm proud to say.

He spoke sparingly. My questions were longer than the answers they elicited from him.

And he was cryptic at best. His responses were vague. Like the ramblings of a mad person. They probably made a whole lot of sense to him, the way he viewed them and how one trail of thought triggered another memory, how one recounting helped him make sense of a different incident altogether, but it took several questions on my part and several retellings on his for me to be able to piece together a coherent story. One that made sense to me.

From what I could gather, the Ahlgrens, who were his ancestors, and the Classions, who were mine, had owned two neighbouring farms in this region. Farmlands that had rolled for acres and acres until the horizon. Friends through several generations, they had been inseparable until a Classion had betrayed an Ahlgren. At this juncture, the strange man, whose name was Marcus Ahlgren, hastened to warn me that if I were to ask a Classion, they'd claim exactly the opposite.

No one in the past seven generations over which this story unfolded had ever discerned the truth. With every retelling, the tale took on more and more of the wrath of the one who told it, the one who felt betrayed, because whether you asked an Ahlgren or a Classion, each felt their family had been not in the wrong but was the wronged one instead.

But what happened next was indisputable, Marcus claimed, noting that I too had seen a version of it unfold with my own eyes. One of his ancestors, an Ahlgren, not even fifteen years old at the time, had been injured in a riding accident and had come stumbling through the woods to the nearest abode he could find. Which, to his saddest misfortune, happened to be the Classions' property.

He had knocked on their door, bloodied and breathless, and tumbled into the house when they had opened the door. The men of the Classion clan had wanted nothing to do with the wounded Ahlgren, but it was the domineering matriarch who had demanded he be let in.

He's only a boy. He's dying, for heavens' sake, she had yelled at her sons.

Let him die then, they had bellowed back at her, for not even fear of falling out of their beloved mother's grace could surpass the hatred that burned and raged in their bellies for the Ahlgrens.

Grudgingly, they had carried him in and laid him on a couch in the living room, where he had sputtered and struggled for barely a few moments. Not enough time for the Classions to settle their debate on whether or not to help the dying Ahlgren in their midst. And he had given up the ghost.

Which had sowed the second seed of dissent in the Classion household that evening. What were they do with the corpse? Ought they to inform the Ahlgrens? That one of theirs had died in an enemy's abode? The consequences of such a deed would be terrible, they feared.

It was evident, even to the kind-hearted matriarch, that the Ahlgrens were unlikely to believe the Classions' version of the events that had transpired. On the contrary, the Ahlgrens would suspect that one of theirs had died at the hands of a Classion. Much bloodshed would ensue within the two families, whatever camaraderie they had once shared now long forgotten; whatever little restraint they had since exercised to keep from going at each other's throats would be obliterated.

There was only one thing to be done. The Classion men carried the dead Ahlgren deep into their neck of the woods and dug a grave for him, deeper than they had ever dug for any of their own, on the highest spot they could find, overlooking the Ahlgren farm.

They said a prayer for him, the kind they did when one of their own died for they knew not any other words to utter at a burial. They gathered wildflowers under the watchful but indifferent gaze of the moon and placed them atop the boy's grave.

And then they went back home, their arms weary from all the digging, their hearts thumping with the knowledge of what they had done, of all the secrets they'd have to carry to their own graves.

Not a word was breathed inside the Classion household about the dead Ahlgren boy. While the men had gone to bury him, the women had scrubbed and polished the floors, washed the blood-soaked velvet fabric of the couch on which the Ahlgren boy had breathed his last without uttering a word on what had brought him to such a tragic end. And they prayed for it to rain that night.

Thunder bellowed and lightning threatened to scorch their land as if the skies too had been furious at such an untimely death. The wrath of nature was such that the Classions almost forgot that the demise of the Ahlgren boy hadn't been their fault. They couldn't be blamed for it, yet they feared punishment for hiding his fate from his family.

In the morning, however, they were only relieved to find that the downpour had washed away every trace of the boy in their fields. No bloody trails, no footprints to suggest an Ahlgren boy had blundered his way into the Classion home and given up the ghost there.

What followed was a manhunt of unprecedented proportions launched by the Ahlgren clan. They scoured every inch of their village and the neighbouring areas for any trace of their lost boy. His horse turned up at the Ahlgren home three days after it had disappeared along with their boy. But its reappearance gave them no clue as to what may have happened to its rider.

The family promised a very generous reward for any information whatsoever on their boy's whereabouts. Sightings were reported, which were undoubtedly false, but only the Classions knew the truth. Swindlers looking to make a quick buck concocted the most unlikely of stories, rekindling hope in the hearts of the Ahlgrens and sending them on a wild goose chase all over again.

Torn by grief, the boy's mother howled a curse into the Universe condemning those involved, whether guilty or not, to a fate worse than death. The loss of their own firstborn child, and that of every firstborn child in their families for generations to come.

A loss too distressful to cope with, and yet they'd have no memory of it whatsoever. All they'd be left with was a long-ing, a great sorrow, with no explanation as to its origins, and with no cure.

And as for the child? Only the child would remember. And the child would lead a life, invisible to their family, pining for a reunion, a chance to be seen, to be heard, to be understood, to be reunited, a chance always out of reach for they were forever forgotten by their own kith and kin.

"THIS IS PRECISELY why the world is completely fucked up," I snorted when Marcus Ahlgren finished his story. I looked at him out of the corner of my eye to see if he had anything to say about my use of foul language, but he didn't, and so I continued, "We are still living out the consequences of the stupid deeds of our great-great-great-great-I-don't-know-how-many-greats-grandparents instead of living our own lives."

He grunted; whether in agreement or not I couldn't tell. For a while, we sat staring at the lavender plants as the breeze ruffled their heads and they leaned towards the ground, having learnt from birth that the best course of action was to stay out of the way of a persistent wind. The sun still hung overhead like a broken clock, clinging to the wrong time.

It occurred to me that the mother of the unfortunate Ahlgren boy had no way to know that her words would bind the Classions in an eternal curse. Had she known that the

Classion family was involved, she would have wished them greater harm.

But what greater torment could there be than the insistent presence of raw, unadorned grief without a reason to explain it? How do you live with sorrow that has no rhyme no reason, that cannot explain its presence, that precludes any healing precisely because of its inherent mysterious nature?

I remembered Aunt Melissa's inexplicable breakdown on the day my family returned to the city, having literally forgotten me behind at the farmhouse.

"I tried to end it," Marcus said at last.

"How?"

"I never married. And I have no siblings."

He is the last Ahlgren, I realised. He *was* the last Ahlgren. Died a few years ago, he told me. And then he had had to wait for the firstborn in our family to be able to see him.

"Me?" I asked.

He looked at me sadly and shook his head. "There was one that came before you."

CHAPTER 10
THE ONE WHO WAS, THEN WASN'T

W hen she was fifteen years old, Bonnie was erased from existence. At fifteen, Bonnie looked a lot like I did. Even though she had dyed her hair purple and mine was still a natural black. Even though she wore her hair long and it grazed the back of her knees, whereas mine had never travelled past my shoulders.

She appeared now in the two photographs that rested atop the chest of drawers in that room with pastel pink walls in which Uncle Jensen and Aunt Melissa stayed during their farmhouse visits.

Where previously Aunt Melissa had one arm in the air, she now rested a hand on her daughter's shoulder.

Bonnie.

The daughter of Aunt Melissa and Uncle Jensen.

The name that had sprung from Aunt Melissa's lips the last time I spoke with her. Mistakenly, we had decided, for we had not known any better.

Bonnie's lifetime of fifteen years had been wiped off from everyone's minds. But the truth of her presence had rested somewhere deep within Aunt Melissa, trying to wriggle its way out of her subconscious but unable to.

The resemblance between Bonnie and me was unmistakable in the way that first cousins could look alike more than they resembled their parents.

It was there in the way she grinned, with abandon, as if she had not a care in the world, but also in the way she thrust her chin at the photographer, in defiance, as if offering a dare.

It was there in the way her eyes were wide open as she took in every single detail of the world around her.

It was there in the way her head was tilted slightly to the right, a tendency that almost every photographer had sought to correct in me, except no one seemed to have pointed out to Bonnie her imperfection, or if they had, she had chosen to ignore it.

Our likeness was even more evident, startlingly so, in the other photograph taken in the lavender fields last year. Here too she appeared now, as if she had been in the picture all along and we were the ones who had lost all sight of her. Which was true in a very literal sense.

I shared more with her than I did with Zelda and Sara.

Gradually, more and more memories began to resurface. I ran down to the kitchen where, sure enough, pencil marks on the doorframe between the kitchen and the landing marked our heights on our birthdays. Purple lines showed how fast I grew. Pink lines now appeared alongside, reminders of how fast Bonnie had grown.

Had they only just reappeared? Or had they been there all along, beside mine, and we had simply forgotten all about Bonnie, an old curse gripping our family in its own twisted way?

Bonnie. Becca. The alliteration had a lilt to it. As if we had been two peas in a pod.

We were both children of summer, and our birthdays were often celebrated here in the farmhouse.

Now that the memories started to resurface, they wouldn't stop coming.

Photo albums showed up in the backs of cupboards and drawers.

Trinkets from a forgotten childhood appeared in the most unexpected of places.

A pair of identical friendship bracelets hung on a hook by the kitchen door.

A dollhouse, painstakingly built and adorned, turned up in the secret hallway between my room and the twins'.

A memory of listening to Abba on an age-old Walkman, each of us taking turns to wear those coveted headphones, the other pressing her ear to the outside of the contraption, eager to catch even the faintest notes streaming out.

Scarlet-lipped. Mascara-lashed eyes, wide open to take in all the sights the world had to offer. Young girls' dreams. Bodies twisting and curving into new, unfamiliar shapes. In that explosion of shared childhoods, we could not be contained.

EVERYTHING ERASED into non-existence because of a stupid, stupid curse that had plagued both the Ahlgrens and the Classions. Oh, yes! Even the Ahlgrens were not spared the ordeal. In wishing another harm, they too had brought doom upon themselves.

Every time an Ahlgren male died, his spirit found its way to the Classion home in a bizarre re-enactment of the day it had all begun.

Marcus's spirit had come blundering through the woods, wounded, desperate for help, in the same way his ancestor had done generations ago, helpless, and had fallen at the Classions' doorstep.

The way he had been permitted inside, with much reluctance, with much debate over the *right* thing to be done, much disagreement over whether the wounded boy should be seen as a human being from whose body life was fast ebbing away, fast receding into that dark space of death, of oblivion, or whether he was to be treated as an Ahlgren, an enemy to be ousted forever, a traitor never to be trusted, never to be aided.

Marcus had only been in his mid-thirties at the time of his death. Nothing spectacular about his passing away. Except, perhaps, his age. His spirit, like those of so many Ahlgren men who had lived and died before he was even born, was compelled to retrace his ancestor's journey to the Classion household, like a pilgrimage, a rite of passage, and remind the Classions yet again of what their predecessors had done. And in so doing, his spirit had found and laid eyes upon the first-born of each Classion family of our generation.

That was the moment, Marcus told me, my family had started to forget about me. The instant he saw me. The instant I saw him emerge from the woods while my sisters and I splashed about in the stream.

That was the moment the unravelling had begun. Every thread of memory was pulled loose from wherever memories were stored. In the mind. In the body. In the heart. From photos and videos. From official records.

Like colours being washed away from a painting left out in the rain. A blurring. An incoherence. Until they bled into each other, into a vague, unappealing grey.

Leaving behind a void.

A Bonnie-shaped hole.

A Becca-shaped hole.

Holes that sucked the very air Mom or Aunt Melissa breathed, leaving them gasping for breath.

Holes that made Dad or Uncle Jensen bury themselves in work in a misguided attempt to soothe their aching hearts.

Holes that would soon send Zelda and Sara looking for love in all the wrong places, in all the wrong people, in all the wrong things.

Holes that would never be filled.

CHAPTER II
THE GIFT OF CLEAR SIGHT

"I should have gone by now," Marcus said to me, a few days after the revelation.

We were walking in the fields. The setting sun made the sky blush. Time had taken to flowing once more, no longer bound by a secret.

Marcus and I lived like ghosts. Which was fine by him, for he was truly dead after all.

I, on the other hand, simply left no impression wherever I went.

Farmhands on the fields would catch a glimpse of me but before they could raise their hands in greeting, they'd lose sight of me. I'd still be there, only invisible to their eyes.

A moment of discombobulation. That's all it would ever cost them. Something to be blamed on the trick of the light. An overworked body. An overactive imagination. A bird, perhaps. Or a dragonfly. A shimmering, glittering speck of something that briefly caught the light of the sun, and then disappeared to wherever the creatures of nature went to hide.

The footprints I made on the mud erased themselves in a

matter of moments. Blades of grass I stepped upon righted themselves almost immediately after I lifted my foot.

This near invisibility could have converted me into a skilled criminal. Theft. Murder. Arson. There was no crime I could be accused of. I didn't stay in people's memories long enough to be captured and punished.

Which was just as well, I thought, the first time it occurred to me that I might have to stock up the pantry if I was doomed to non-exist here for the remainder of this pitiful excuse for a life. But turned out, even hunger and thirst had left me to my own devices.

It was as if I had become only as real, or as unreal, as an amalgamation of every memory of me ever held by anyone. Wiped out of everybody's memories, I didn't quite exist.

The thought that Marcus, the only person who could see me and sit beside me and talk and laugh and cry with me, would have to go away too hadn't occurred to me until he brought it up. The prospect of yet another abandonment so soon felt as if an arrow had made its way through my heart and beyond.

"Gone where?" I asked.

"Wherever the souls of the dead go."

"Then why haven't you?"

He didn't answer for a while, so I stopped strolling and turned around to face him. He looked in the distance and answered, without meeting my eyes, "Because there may be more."

"More what?"

"More firstborn Classions to … to …"

Even after all these years, I wondered what his first choice of word would have been. To eliminate? To dispense with? To get rid of? To be disposed of? Like trash?

I knew I wasn't being kind to him. After all, it wasn't his fault that a loony ancestor of his had chosen to make life miserable for everyone who had had the misfortune to be born in either of the two families. And Marcus had done his part by not marrying, by not spawning more Ahlgrens for their spirits to carry out the monstrous task of wiping out another human's existence.

Yet, I couldn't stem the tide of viciousness that longed to erupt out of me like a volcano, scorching and dissolving everything that came in its way, burning everything into crumbly, flaky ash.

"More firstborn Classions to what, Marcus?" I yelled, jabbing a finger at him. "To make disappear? To be torn apart from their families? To be yanked out of life and thrown into a living death?"

IT TOOK me four days to stop wallowing in my own misery and set out in search of Marcus after that conversation. He had not deigned to answer my question that evening. He had simply walked off into the woods, and I had chosen to stomp back home where I had plenty of opportunities to discover even more aspects of the human life that had been snatched away from me.

Words I wrote on a piece of paper disappeared as if written with vanishing ink.

Melodies I sang out loud did not fall upon another's ears.

Occasionally, I'd sneak up on a farmhand or one of the

high school brats who manned the gift shop and scream *'Boo'* into their ears. Sure enough they'd snap their head around, their attention registering my presence for barely an instant, before they'd turn back to the cash register they were manning or the shelves they were stocking or the blooms they were plucking, having unknowingly lost a couple of moments of their life to the eccentricities of a non-being.

Books were the only companions that did not fail me. Every story I read stayed with me long after I had finished reading it. But then the prospect of sitting with myself, with memories and regrets only I held, with my remembrances of the people who had forgotten all about me, was too bleak to bear. And so I reached for the next book on the shelf, whether it was a love story, or a saga about a battle unfolding in the space between midnight stars, or a detailed description of the human anatomy, and I read indiscriminately.

Until I ran out of books to read anew and had to contend with the irrevocable truth that this was it. This was my life now. Or non-life. A quasi-existence. Neither alive nor dead, for all practical purposes.

I was already losing so much of myself, of what I had known and embodied in my human existence, that I told myself it was the fear of losing Marcus and finding myself all alone in this state of quasi-existence that had wrenched the bitterness out of me and put it on display. But it had hurt him, I could tell, to be accused of the crimes his forebears had perpetrated, the price for which he was still paying.

Besides, I had nothing else to do but sit by the stream or in the fields and watch life make its way all around me. And so I set out into the woods in search of him.

The woods had always been out of bounds for the three—

no, four—of us. We weren't allowed to venture here without a grown-up accompanying us. It wasn't a directive we were particularly keen to disobey, especially after the ghost stories Dad and Uncle Jensen used to tell us every night we spent here at the farmhouse, each trying to outdo the other when it came to striking terror in our hearts, no doubt in an attempt to dissuade us from running off into the woods all by ourselves and getting hopelessly lost there.

But safety was no longer a matter of concern for me, I realised that morning as I began to walk beside the stream, making my way in the direction opposite to her flow.

The sight of plump, black mulberries made my throat water, stirring a recent memory of their juicy sweetness. I plucked one and nibbled on it, knowing quite well what to expect but hoping against hope for a miracle. It tasted of nothing. I dropped it to the ground, where it rolled away in a carpet of ripe fruits that ought to have filled the air with their sweetness but hadn't.

Scent was one human characteristic that remained for the most part, although it too occasionally eluded me. The memories of certain scents, especially that of lavender, were still imprinted in my mind though.

Closing my eyes, I thought of the farm and the countless times my sisters and I had traipsed through the rows and rows of blooming flowers, their heady fragrance an indispensable part of our breath.

I could almost feel the tickle in the back of my throat that the first whiff of lavender often brought on. But how was I to know if it was merely my mind playing tricks on me or a reality I had been able to conjure up from memory?

Even more startling was the discovery that this realisation

did not fling me into a depressed, desperate state of mind. As if I had adapted to this new way of being in a matter of days.

A pair of mallard ducks, a male and a female, glided down the stream. Their special purple-blue strips tucked within their plumage occasionally gleamed in the light of the sun. I stopped to watch them as they paused every so often, pecking for food here and there, upending to scour the bottom of the stream for delicacies, then moved on, looking out for each other in unspoken harmony.

Sunlight and leaf-shadow played all around me. Tall pines and maples and spruces grew uninhibitedly. Cardinals, common blackbirds, blue jays, and sparrows called and chirped and twittered from perches hidden inside bushes.

Like little children playing a game of hide-and-seek but unable to contain their giggles, only too happy to give themselves away.

Behind me, the farmhouse was no longer visible.

At first.

All I could see were the greens and browns of large, towering trees, archetypes of the earth herself rising on the strength of their own form to seek and kiss the drifting clouds above, coaxing them to stay, to give up the precious moisture they threatened to carry away to distant lands, and empty themselves of their burdens here, now, to quench this land's insatiable thirst.

The farmhouse was hidden behind this drama of life unfolding in front of my eyes. I couldn't see it at first, but the more I looked, the more it revealed itself. An outline at first. Then a solid shape. And then the colours filling themselves in. Red roofs, parched by the sun into a dusty sienna. White walls. Red doors. Windows wide open. The lavender fields adjoining the house and the woods. The gift shop. Busier than usual today, business brisker now that the end of the season was almost upon us and summer was slipping away, dragging along with it the opportunity to brag about a visit to a lavender farm. Or the chance to purchase exquisite products. Lavender-scented memorabilia. Something to help remember the past when the present became too difficult to live in.

I could see the stream meander through the woods, bending and curving this way and that, deceptively calm and docile, seemingly with no complaints about the obstacles that constantly showed up but, in its own manner, eroding and devouring everything that once stood in its way. Past hurts never forgotten. Past slights avenged eventually.

In the distance, the lake gleamed. A thin strip of blue, sunlight striking its surface and converting its own reflection in each drop of water into elusive jewels.

I turned back to face the direction I had been headed in before my brief pause. With my eyes, I followed the path of the stream, up a gentle slope, water jumping over rocks and boulders like pups frolicking and bounding down a grassy slope, branching out at various points in the distance into the small trickles that came together to form a unified force of nature.

Where I had become near invisible to the world, I had also been blessed with the clarity of sight. Everything in that space between me and the horizon glowed, as if especially for me, wanting to be seen and acknowledged and admired.

And unfettered by the very human constraints of thirst and hunger, fear of pain or death, fear of being wrong or rejected, I walked. Chin up, chest out, head held high. Eager to see and observe, watch and absorb every detail of this world around me, without having to care what it meant for me, without fearing how any of it would affect me and my quasi-life.

For the first time in my ordeal, I came to appreciate the unprecedented liberation it offered me. In being excluded from the living world, I had somehow become more of a part of it. I could see more of it from the outside than I had been able to from within.

The world was more willing to offer up its secrets to me now that I had no need or use for them. I was no longer a threat, and so I could be trusted.

Giddy with this discovery, I ploughed on, feeling the way my boot-clad feet pressed on the ground under which creatures of the soil wriggled and squirmed and the roots of trees passed on secret messages to each other far and wide.

It no longer mattered that I'd be obliterated from their memories even before I had taken the next step. The sights presented to me rid me of my own desperation to be seen. When there were so many sights to soak up in this world of ours, there was little time to be wasted in the inane pursuit of being seen and admired.

It was this gift that helped me spot Marcus that morning. He was several kilometres away, sitting under a massive oak tree atop a small hill, leaning against its trunk, looking out into the distance. I followed his gaze and even though he was looking somewhere I couldn't immediately spot, it only took me a few moments to see through all the foliage and the rise and fall of the land to discern what must have once been the home of the Ahlgrens.

A farmhouse, that would have once been like ours, barring the gaping holes where the roof had caved in and the windows had fallen out, and the creepers crawling up the walls like hands reaching out of the ground to claim the structure as their own. Surrounding it was a vast field of weeds and wildflowers.

Even from this distance the place appeared deserted, abandoned long ago by the humans who must have lived and loved there once.

"The last of the Ahlgrens lived there more than a century ago," Marcus said as I approached him.

I kept mum. On my way here, it occurred to me that silence, rather than questioning, might prompt him to share more about himself than he otherwise would.

He continued, "My great-grandfather abandoned the farm and moved down south to work in the factories. He thought getting away from the property would put an end to the curse that has plagued our families for generations. It didn't, but at least it was only in death that we had to reckon with what was demanded of our spirits. The lives we lived were free of family secrets and enmity and curses." He sighed.

"I'm so sorry," I said, apologising for all the accusations I had hurled at him when we last met, and also commiserating for the loss he and his family had endured.

He nodded. That was all the forgiveness I was going to receive. That was all the forgiveness needed to put that spat behind us and move on.

"And to think that fifteen-year-old Adrian Ahlgren had been laid to rest right here, beneath this giant oak, giving his remains a clear view of the rest of his family and the generations that followed, of the beloved farm he had grown up in, the farm that would have become his in due course of time."

"This is part of the Ahlgren property?" I asked, surprised.

Marcus nodded. "The truth becomes clear only when we die, because then it is too late to do anything with it."

I jumped up and backed away from the oak tree, peering down at the ground as I stepped back. Whatever elements had once constituted the young Ahlgren lad had long turned into earth and become an indistinguishable part of it.

It must have taken uncanny courage on the part of my Classion ancestors to have buried an Ahlgren in his own land. Trespassing the boundaries that had been erected between the two families who had become embroiled in an irresolvable feud by then, long friendships forgotten, the blemish of betrayal staining whatever camaraderie may have once existed.

Or had the Classions had the last laugh? Knowing that the Ahlgrens would scour the earth, dig every patch of land but their own, in search of their missing lad?

Either way it must have been a risky undertaking. Whether motivated by generosity, a sense of obligation towards a friendship that had blossomed once upon a time, or by a desperate need for survival, a strategy devised to thwart any bloodshed, who could tell after all this time?

This is the thing about stories. They shape-shift all the time. With every retelling, a story reveals something new because you, the reader, the listener, you would have changed. You are no longer the person you were before you heard the story for the first time. It has changed you. And, in turn, you change it too. Perhaps a word gone missing from here. A new turn of phrase added there. Morphing and changing, it is as if the story needed to take a life all of its own.

As had the tale of the Ahlgrens and the Classions.

As had the story of Marcus Ahlgren.

And the story of me, Rebecca Classion.

Known to my family and friends, once upon a time, as Becca.

Now, completely forgotten.

Erased from existence.

CHAPTER 12

INVISIBLE THIEF

As I put my hand out to pull the gate open, Marcus warned me for the umpteenth time that it was a terrible idea and that it still wasn't too late to turn around and head back to the farmhouse.

But I was riding high on a colossal wave of excitement, even with him sounding like a broken record throughout the journey, and I wasn't about to turn back now.

You're probably wondering what I'm prattling on about. I'm getting ahead of myself, I know, I know.

So the first thing I ought to mention—the very thing that turned everything on its head yet again—was that I discovered that I could now travel beyond the confines of the Classion and the Ahlgren lands.

The last time I had stepped outside the gates of the farmhouse, the road outside had led me back to the one place I had been trying to get away from.

When I had learnt the truth and, more importantly, come to accept my fate, those constraints had disappeared, Marcus explained, well aware of what I'd likely do next even though he promptly warned me against it.

Realising that nothing now stopped me from paying a visit to my family, I had run outside in the middle of the night before, eager to find a taxi or hitch-hike my way to their townhouse, our townhouse, downtown.

It was a futile attempt. There were few vehicles on the road at that time of the night. I had positioned myself under the brightest streetlamp I could find to make myself easily visible.

Trouble was it didn't help me regain visibility in the sense that mattered. Every time a vehicle appeared in the distance heading my way, I jumped up and down and waved my arms over my head.

On every occasion, the vehicle slowed down, as if the driver had noticed me, but just as I'd prepare to walk up to them and request a ride, they'd simply rev up and speed away, unable to see any longer whatever or whoever had drawn their attention momentarily.

Marcus had watched me for a while with amusement but had eventually drawn my attention to the fact that my parents and sisters were only likely to be terrified if I were to ring their doorbell or knock on their door in the dead of night. He had a point.

And so I had spent a rather restless night, not even attempting to invite sleep knowing it would remain stubbornly elusive until I made this trip. I had paced up and down my room, trying to come up with a plan that didn't entail me having to walk all the way to our downtown home, until I realised that I was only working myself up to a frenzy by moving without pause and gave myself permission to sit down with a book on my lap and scanned the first page over and over again without registering any of the words on it.

If you had asked me then, I would have promised you that I held no illusion of a reunion with my parents and my sisters, and that I had braced myself to face their unawareness of my existence. Falser words were never spoken.

When dawn broke, I showered and wore a white summer dress with a floral print, in lavender, of course, which Mom and Dad had gifted me last year. I chose this dress in the hope, although Marcus had warned me from asking for the impossible, that if not my face, at least my dress would trigger a long-forgotten memory in them.

I went easy on the makeup knowing how much Mom disapproved of it. *You're too young*, she'd shake her head, as if only grown-ups were meant to have the privilege of concealing one's true face from the world around them.

A tender wave of affection swelled in my heart and tears rolled down my cheeks before I even realised what was happening. I sat on the edge of the bed, gripped in an agony stronger than I had felt on that afternoon when I had woken up to find my family had left without me.

Conversing with Marcus and discovering and employing my new gift of clear sight had rendered the past several days more than bearable, enjoyable even. But now the memories of my last interactions with Zelda and Sara, Mom and Dad, Uncle Jensen and Aunt Melissa, burst into my head all at once like a dam giving way, breached by the very waters it was meant to contain in safety.

It was the thought that Marcus would once again try to dissuade me from undertaking this endeavour that finally made me pull myself together, erase all traces of grief and tears from my face, and step out where he was waiting at his usual perch, on the topmost patio step.

In the brief time I had known him, he hadn't entered the farmhouse, although I reckoned he could have, being a ghost or a spirit or whatever label he chose for himself.

But he hadn't transgressed that unspoken boundary thus far, and I found some solace in the fact that the person who was responsible, directly or indirectly, for my separation from the rest of my family did not invite himself into an abode that still rang with the laughter of my sisters, was full of the aroma of Mom's cooking, and hummed with the memories of generations of Classions who had either lived here for all their lives or had made occasional visits to the property, often enough to have created fond memories to reminisce upon.

Marcus had taken one look at my face and shaken his head again. I looked towards the fields where the sun shone brilliantly on the lavender blooms. The breeze was cool and gentle, giving away no indication of the heat that was to follow later in the day.

I took all these as signs to follow my heart's whim, to do what made my heart sing, even if I had to spend the rest of my life collecting the countless pieces it was about to be shattered into. I was a woman with a plan that morning, and nothing could deter me.

Outside the gates, Marcus propped himself up on one of a handful of boulders that rose from the ground near the entrance and settled down for another round of entertainment.

I smirked inwardly and picked up a stone so large and heavy I needed both hands to carry it without losing my balance. At the sight of the first car headed south, I planted myself in the middle of the opposite lane with my back towards the house and Marcus, so I could keep an eye on my unsuspecting ride into town as well as on any vehicles coming the other way up the lane I was standing in. Near invisibility didn't guarantee me immunity from death, I was pretty certain.

It was a nondescript white SUV. The kind a soccer mom uses to shuttle her three or more kids to various activities in a bid to keep them engaged while she waited in her car, sometimes busy, sometimes bored, often wondering who she even was when she wasn't looking after her children.

I held my breath and waited, hoping no children were travelling in the car that fateful morning. Luck favoured me. A young woman was the only occupant of the vehicle.

As the SUV drew nearer, she flicked a glance at me. Her momentary sighting of me before I became unseeable to her.

When the car was almost beside me, I lifted the rock above my head and flung it with all my might on its bonnet.

At the unexpected crash of stone on metal, the driver briefly lost control and the car careened to the side of the lane it was on, screeching to a halt as the driver slammed on the brakes, instinctively responding to the external impact on the vehicle. She sat there, stunned for an instant.

I ran up to her as she opened her door and tumbled out, shocked and a little disoriented. I scanned her for any signs of injury, but she appeared unharmed, bodily at least.

"Are you hurt?" I asked, drawing her attention to me, albeit for only a fleeting instant.

She shook her head, then moved away towards the front of the car to see what had crashed into the vehicle, worried at what she may find.

There was nothing.

In the few moments that had elapsed since the impact, it had all been undone. Yet another act of mine gently erased from the face of this world, all traces of it eliminated as surely as the incident was quickly fading from the driver's memory.

Her forehead was no longer scrunched up with worry. Instead, she stood, scratching her head, running her fingers through hair that had appeared raven black at first but gleamed with hints of midnight blue in the sunlight.

Her phone lay in the passenger seat. I grabbed it and pressed the Emergency call button, which connected the phone to the local emergency services without demanding a password.

"911. Police, fire, or ambulance?"

I almost whooped when I heard the operator's voice on the other end. "Police, please," I yelled into the phone.

This drew the attention of the driver, who had been checking under the car and around it with bewilderment plastered on her face. She looked up sharply at me, wondering where I had turned up from.

Relief and wariness fought to express themselves on her face. Relief that I might be able to help. Wariness at my abrupt appearance. Like a genie from a bottle. I only had a split second to act.

I set the phone on speaker mode and thrust it into her hand. "Here," I said, "I dialled 911 for help."

She took her phone from my hand, surprised at the sight of her own phone being handed to her but also accepting the wisdom of reaching out to 911 for help, whether or not she had a reason.

"Hello," she mumbled into her phone, holding its mic end close to her mouth, unsure of what to say.

"Yes, ma'am," the operator's voice came through, loud and clear. Patient. Waiting. "What's your emergency?"

"Emergency?" The woman looked at me as if seeking a cue. I didn't give her any. At least, not right then.

I backed away from her slowly. The voice from the phone persisted in its demand for an answer. The woman tried desperately to come up with something that sounded sane at least to her own ears. She looked from her phone to her car. I had become invisible to her once more.

"What's your emergency, ma'am?"

"I'm not really sure," the woman said at last.

It was now or never. I jumped into the driver's seat and slammed the door shut, turned on the ignition, swerved the car well away from the driver, who was now thoroughly startled and broke into a run after me.

I almost collided with an oncoming truck, which veered away from me and towards the boulders where Marcus had sat only moments ago, giving me enough room to manoeuvre the SUV back into the correct lane without running the driver down.

I tore down the street towards my family's home downtown, with Marcus sitting beside me, shaking his head and grinning in disbelief. This was probably the most excitement he'd had in a very long time.

I glanced at the rear-view mirror. Already the truck I had nearly rammed into was far receding into the distance. The driver of the SUV I had stolen and was now driving was merely a speck on the horizon. Finally, I had given the unfortunate and completely befuddled woman a reason to have called 911.

Not that anyone would remember seeing me fly down the road, breaking every rule of the road, not even having a licence in the first place, and exercising caution only to avoid collisions. I faced no risk of being caught. None whatsoever. But I was still aware that invisibility did not mean immortality, and this was not the time to die.

My driving ability was not in the question. Dad had taught me how to drive when I was fourteen. The roads around our farm were mostly deserted. This morning was perhaps the first time a police car had been called to attend to an incident there.

Navigating the traffic was hardly unnerving. What worried me more was that the momentary sight of me might distract other drivers and lead them straight into inexplicable accidents. But the journey passed without incident, much to my relief. The Classions didn't need to bear responsibility for yet another death, directly or indirectly.

Easing into downtown, I slowed down to take in the familiar sights and sounds. Marcus too looked around, hungrily devouring the images of life around him.

I rolled down the windows. The overpowering smell of exhaust fumes and stress with undertones of coffee and the heady scents of expensive perfumes mingling with those of cheap deodorants wafted into our car.

I shook my head at my choice of words. *Our car?* Only a few minutes had passed since I'd procured the vehicle by not entirely legal means, and I was already laying claim to it.

It must be a weekday, I remember thinking as I slowed down. Without a routine to hold on to, the days had segued into each other back at the farmhouse. But here, officegoers in smart suits walked briskly in formal shoes, juggling coffee cups and laptop bags or files or other important-looking paraphernalia, and wearing harassed expressions on their faces.

If it was a weekday, the twins would be getting ready to go to summer camp. Dad would have left for work already, prone as he was to begin his day even before the sun rose.

I parked the SUV in a designated spot a few blocks away from home, and hoped the vehicle would soon be reunited with its owner.

As I stepped out, a current of nervous energy shot up my spine. Ever since the possibility had presented itself to me, I had been in no doubt about finding a way to come downtown and see my family once again.

But now that I was here, I found it hard to be intentional about the purpose of this visit. What did I want out of this?

I was already prepared for their inability to perceive or recognise me. They wouldn't even register my presence for longer than a moment or two. I knew better than to harbour any hopes of a jovial reunion. Then what was I here for? Was it curiosity? Some unfinished business?

I stole a sideways look at Marcus who was walking beside me, gaping open-mouthed at the bustle of life around him. He was still around, his spirit cursed to prise yet another first-born Classion before he could stop haunting the world of the living and make his way to wherever the souls of the dead went.

Suddenly, bringing him right to my family's doorstep didn't seem like a grand idea. What if his presence caused them some harm? What if Zelda, the older of the twins, were to notice him and be condemned to a fate like mine? But she wasn't a firstborn. That soothed my nerves somewhat.

Gah! Now that the excitement of setting out on this expedition had died down, I couldn't muster the gumption to actually walk down my street—my street, hah!—and up the few steps that lay between me and the door of my home. Again, that possessive determiner. My. Mine. Me. When everything could be, and had indeed been, snatched away from me in an instant.

For all the bravado I tried to portray, pretending complete acceptance of the inevitable indifference I'd face from Mom and the twins for no fault of theirs, I was still unsure what events this brazen act of mine was about to set into motion.

"I'd better stay here," Marcus said in a low voice, nudging me out of my reverie. It was only then that I noticed we were outside my home. A modern brick-and-stone townhouse, it was quite indistinguishable from the five houses that hugged it on either side. Right down to the black door, the gleaming brass knob and door knocker, and even the black metal railings that flanked the five steps leading up to the cosy porch landing.

I must have been four years old when we moved in here. All the houses looked alike, barring the ones at the two ends. I remember asking Mom how I'd know which our home was, as if even then I had somehow doubted my ability to find my way back home in a time of need. She pointed to the number 321 in brass lettering that shone above the door knocker. "Easy to remember, isn't it?" she had asked with a bright smile on her face. I must have not mirrored her confidence, for she scooped me up in her arms and, hugging me tightly, said, "Even if you don't remember, it's quite alright. You'll never have to find your way back home alone. A grown-up will always be with you."

Even with the house number to guide us, we eventually found little markers to identify our home. Our gate had a second latch at the top, out of reach of our little arms. And then there was that loose brick on the pavement outside the house two doors before ours. No one really knew whose responsibility it was to get it fixed, so it remained wobbly to this day. And the house right after ours had a coral bark Japanese maple, which provided an unmissable landmark.

All those signs were there that day when I returned home in a car I had stolen with much ingenuity given my situation and abilities or lack thereof. I looked up at the sky, a bright blue hemmed in by the roofs of townhouses and apartment buildings huddled together, as if for warmth and comfort, in the city. Only small patches of blue visible to those who managed to drag themselves away from the plethora of sights that fought for their attention on the ground.

I had almost put my hand on the gate, ignoring Marcus's incessant pleas to turn back, when the door was pulled open and out tumbled Zelda, followed by Sara, followed by Mom. Three peas in a pod. Almost triplets. So alike they looked. I gasped. The twins looked up.

This was it.

The moment of truth.

The moment of reckoning.

I stood, frozen in place, unable to feel my legs beneath me, let alone will them to whisk me away from here, from now.

And then they waved.

"Beck!" they called out as they came bounding down the stairs.

CHAPTER 13

OLD HAUNTS, NEW LIVES

Forbidden hope bloomed from deep within me and I permitted it to inundate me, engulf me, whisk me away into a whirlwind of unbelievable joy. Dare I say it? A miracle come true!

"Zelda! Sara!" I called out as tears ran down my cheeks.

But my voice was drowned by another's. Shriller. More ecstatic. Zelda prised the gate open and stepped on it to swing it open. I stumbled back, hastily out of the way.

"Sorry," Zelda said, noticing me for a split second, forgetting me the very next instant, her attention already drawn towards another girl getting out of a car on the road behind me. Zelda jumped off the gate as the girl, the one and only Beck who mattered, stepped out of her chauffeur-driven Audi, and exchanged air-kisses with my sister.

Oh! I knew her. Not Beck. But Beth! Lisbeth! Elizabeth, actually. A hoity-toity girl in the twins' class who found her legal name too old-fashioned and had spun something more modern, more fashionable out of it.

I thought the twins hated her. Why was Zelda air-kissing

her and getting into the car beside her? Giggling and squirming, twisting her body this way and that and twirling her hair around her fingers? Acting like a girly girl? Like the girl she absolutely was not?

I turned back and looked at Mom, aghast. But Mom had a beatific smile on her face, delighting in the transformation of her daughter from wild girl to graceful lady, pleased with the induction of her daughter into the upper echelons of society.

A feather-light touch on the back of my arm made me spin around again. There was Sara, walking quietly around the back of the car to the other side. She pulled the door open, then waved to Mom whose attention had been freed from Zelda's grip, now that the older twin was ensconced in the backseat with her new bestie, Lisbeth. Mom waved back to Zelda.

My youngest sister then turned her head and looked at me squarely for a moment. As if she could see me. Before I could react, she turned away and let her gaze rest on something in the distance. I followed her line of sight and found Marcus, leaning against a length of black metal fencing in front of the adjoining house, watching this family drama unfold with deep sadness. Could she see him? Impossible!

"Hurry up, Sara! Stop dawdling!" Zelda's voice came from inside the car, shrill and insistent as ever.

Sara turned from Marcus to look at me again for a moment that stretched into eternity. And then she gave me the tiniest of shrugs. A shrug, nonetheless. Then a sigh. And she slid down and into the car in one swift motion and pulled the door shut behind her. The car pulled away with the three girls in the backseat, Sara attached to Zelda's side like an auxiliary limb, one that could be discarded without any significant consequence whenever the situation demanded.

Mom came down the steps as the girls were whisked away to wherever they had planned this one of the last few days of their summer holidays. The gate had been left open and Mom moved to draw it shut. I slipped inside before she could register my presence as anything more than a breath or a sigh or a whiff of a stranger's perfume.

I ran up the steps and entered my once-upon-a-time home. So little had changed. Yet everything felt both familiar and somehow distant at the same time. A reminder of the transient nature of everything. What had once been indisputably mine, no longer was.

Slippers and shoes spilled out everywhere from the closet by the door, the remnants, no doubt, of a frantic search by the twins for their particular pairs without which they wouldn't have wanted to leave from home. None were mine.

The pictures in the hallway clung to the wall as they always had, in sets of four forming a diamond-like shape, with every trace of me erased.

What never was, will never be.

Like a moth to a flame, I was drawn towards all the places from where I had been obliterated.

In the kitchen, where I had once painted lavender blooms on the corners of cupboard doors as a summer project. No visitor to our home had passed this way without noticing and admiring the intricate design. Now, the doors were a naked white. No distinguishing features to remind the Classions of a daughter and her artistic impulses.

Upstairs. I first entered the twins' room. The scent of lavender mingled with the chemical fragrance of nail paints and sweet-smelling lotions, the exotic perfume of old paper and new books collided in mid-air and settled upon every surface. The bunk beds. Tables and chairs. Chests of drawers. The dollhouse. Two separate lives crammed into a room too small to contain them together any longer.

Hand on my throat, I made my way to what used to be my room. The door was closed. I put my hand on the knob but couldn't bring myself to twist it and push the door open. The sound of another door closing downstairs. Mom must have come back into the house. It was just the impetus I needed. My hand twisted the doorknob of its own accord and my feet carried me into what had once been the room of my childhood.

In my memory, my room was my definition of heaven. Deep purple walls on one of which I had taped larger-than-life-sized posters of The Cranberries, No Doubt, and Roxette. From the opposite wall, Abba, Ace of Base, The Carpenters, Mariah Carey, and Whitney Houston looked at me, their eyes sombre and challenging, daring me to dream bigger dreams for myself than I could wrap my head around, each one in their own perfect way.

Between these two walls dedicated to the singers whose music had given me whole new perspectives on life, my bed had stood with bright red covers and a pale pink, almost colourless, blanket of fleece. A favourite I had held on to for more than a decade, I had often been told.

I still remembered the entire wall's length of worktops and shelves that Dad had had custom-built around the only window in the room, giving me a pleasing view of treetops as I hunched over my homework, and plenty of space to store everything I used or needed, from my schoolwork to my art projects, from mixtape cassettes to the one and only tube of lipstick I was permitted to own after I had entered my teens.

In the reality that presented itself to me, the room was a liminal space. An abode in transition. Much of it was featureless. Bare walls in the colour of sand. A lone bed in the centre, like an oasis, draped in soft pink linen. A chest of drawers tucked under the window. A room held for guests, perhaps. For temporary visitors who wanted neither their host's personal tastes to be thrust upon them nor to leave behind any mark of their own.

I stepped in and looked around. Four stripes of paint marred the wall beside the door. Like a multicoloured scratch made by claws on a face. Rich burgundy. Cornflower blue. Seawater teal. Rich, royal purple. As if someone had been testing the different shades of colours to paint the wall in.

It was the purple that startled me. I could have sworn it was the same shade the walls of my room had once been bathed in. As I moved towards the wall for a closer look, something appeared in the corner of my eye. I bent to peek under the bed. Peeking back at me was a pair of black sandals with golden glitter and inch-long heels. One of the twins', undoubtedly. But which one's?

On an impulse, I headed towards the chest of drawers and pulled the top drawer open gently, trying not to make any sound. It slid easily and revealed, all too eagerly, a diary with a lock and a pen tucked into an attached holder.

I checked the lower drawers one by one. A hair clip made of sequins. A bow that seemed to have fallen out of the band or clip it had once been a part of, the patch of dried glue still clinging to it on the rear side. A stuffed pup holding a heart-shaped plushy in its mouth. I remembered this one very well.

It had been Mom's Valentine's gift to the twins earlier this year. Mom had bought a pair of identical soft toys for the girls. I had thought they were too old for plushies, but Mom was adamant that girls never outgrew their need for soft toys. Looking back now, I think it was Mom who did not want her girls to grow up too fast. She'd have wanted them to stay little girls forever. But the twins were ecstatic at the sight of their identical gifts. Until one of the stuffed pups went missing within the week and neither Zelda nor Sara could agree on who had lost their gift.

The pup that remained lay on its back in the bottommost drawer, still claimed by both the girls as theirs, the last I knew. Perhaps, that too had changed. Maybe one of the twins, and my bet was on Zelda, had decided to draw a boundary of separation between them. A clear demarcation of what belonged to whom, who belonged to which room. For this old room of mine was certainly being spruced up to soon become another's, I was beginning to see.

The one question I couldn't answer though was this: whose? Was it Zelda who was giving up the only room she had known all her life in order to stake out new territory? Or was it Sara who was being banished from the only haven she had known all her life and being forced into another world?

Knowing what I knew of my twins, having seen what I had seen of them outside our home a few minutes ago, I was certain that whatever was transpiring here, Zelda had a greater say in it than Sara did. One led. The other followed. It had always been that way. It had never been any other way.

CHAPTER 14

NEWLY FIFTEEN

T*he truth becomes clear when you die. When it is too late to do anything with it.*

In those initial years, I clung to Marcus Ahlgren's words like a mantra. An enlightenment. Something like an absolution, so I wouldn't harass my half-dead soul with all that I could have done, all that could have been, had I only known the truth a little earlier, when I was more alive and able to put it to good use.

But every time Marcus asked me exactly what it was I thought I could have done to alter the way fate was unfolding, I came up empty. Like a fish gasping for breath in mid-air.

FIVE YEARS HAD PASSED since the last time I made my way home.

Five years had passed since the last time the Classion clan made its way to the farmhouse in its entirety.

I saw Grandma and Uncle Jensen once, both having aged

ten years in the five that had passed. It had been a foggy, fall morning.

It was a day I remembered very well. For yet another lavender season had come and gone, and the farmhouse had been left undisturbed. What I gleaned from the hired farmhands was that the family's business interests had diversified so much that they no longer felt compelled to be involved in the day-to-day operations of the farm. That responsibility had been bestowed upon strangers who worked hard and in earnest, contrary to my expectations and much to my disappointment for such a well-run farm needed no direct intervention from Dad or Uncle Jensen. It gave them no reason to visit the farm. Other, more important matters held their attention.

Mom could have come up with the twins though, I argued with myself in my head, feeling let down yet again.

The first year following the erasure of my life had been the hardest. I had hoped Mom and Dad and the twins would come to the farmhouse for yet another weekend getaway that summer. When they didn't, I held out hope for a family visit during the winter holidays.

But even though hired cleaners showed up with annoying regularity throughout the year to scrub the floors and rake the leaves and mow the lawn and shovel the snow and change the sheets and dust the furniture, keeping the property well-maintained enough to accommodate an impromptu visit, no one I knew or cared for or loved, turned up.

"You're taking it personally," Marcus said to me often in the early days.

But even the irrefutable knowledge that nobody could be blamed was not enough to keep me from grieving.

Winters had so far proven to be the hardest. Although the elements couldn't perturb me and I could spend all night lying on the snow under the stars, forming momentary clouds with my breath, some days even the sky hung so low I felt it would squeeze the life out of me.

Autumn quickly became my favourite season. The lavender plants were trimmed, and new seeds were planted well before the first frost. The gift shop was emptied, and all the beautiful items made their way to a little shop downtown where they were sold as holiday gifts. Memories of summer promising to keep you warm through a seemingly endless winter.

It was only when the farm was deserted once more that I could make peace with my state of oblivion. Nothing was worse than feeling lonely and unseen in a crowd.

I was sitting on a rock by the creek that autumn morning, watching the trees drop their leaves everywhere. Bits of scarlet, orange, and yellow fluttered and twirled down to the ground. Some landed on the creek and floated away with the water. I looked into the water and saw beneath its rocky bottom, past the layers of mud and dirt and the roots of trees reaching out to each other, like fingers seeking others like themselves for comfort and companionship, where little animals dug and burrowed and made their homes warm and cosy for the winter.

It was their voices that drifted on the cool breeze and dragged me out of the vision I was lost in. I whipped my head around. Grandma and Uncle Jensen emerged from around the corner of the farmhouse like two unexpected figures wrapped in ribbons of mist.

I almost fell off my perch on the rock, but I quickly

regained my balance and darted across the yard to hide behind the nearest tree, a large sugar maple that continued to drop leaves on my head as if the world had not suddenly been turned and plonked upside down.

My abrupt movement made Grandma and Uncle Jensen look up but only for an instant. Whatever it was they had seen, or thought they had seen, they had already dismissed as a bird in sudden flight or the scamper of a squirrel or the white flash of a rabbit scurrying into the undergrowth.

Uncle Jensen held a small urn in his hands, while Grandma held on to him as they made their way, slow and wobbly, to the creek.

They hadn't entered the house. They must have parked in the driveway and walked around the house to the back. I craned my neck for a clearer look.

When they reached the rock I had been sitting on, Uncle Jensen helped Grandma rest against it. He then opened the lid of the urn. Obsidian black, it gleamed like a small oval of night in his hands. Like the eye of a red cardinal. Bright and beady.

Uncle Jensen sat on his haunches and held out the urn in front of Grandma who grasped it with shaking hands. Uncle didn't let go of the urn but followed Grandma's lead as she leaned forward as far as she could and tipped the urn over the water.

The mortal remains of Grandpa, I now knew, slipped from his last abode, that small black urn, into the creek, where the waters washed him away until he was formless once more. Several specks of ash were caught in the breeze and scattered like tiny insects.

When the deed was done, Grandma sat back and sighed.

Uncle Jensen dipped the urn in the creek, allowing the water to rush in and cleanse out every physical trace of Grandpa. He then placed the urn beside Grandma, walked to the side of the house, and returned with a shovel. The spot he chose was under the very sugar maple tree behind which I hid and watched. He dug a shallow pit and buried the urn in it. Grandma sat by the creek, watching him and the water, occasionally the sky and the falling leaves. The sky was a brilliant blue, the kind of blue you see only in spring and autumn, the kind of blue that glows when the sun isn't hot enough to outshine it. Grandpa would have liked it.

That was more than three seasons ago.

It was an early summer morning. The last of the snow had long melted away from memory and the promise of warmer weather was fulfilled. It was no longer a promise that could be reneged on from the looks of it, even though the weather in these parts was known to spring a nasty surprise when least expected.

The surprise that morning came in another form. The cleaners were here again. That, in itself, wasn't unexpected. They had come only the previous week, as they had every week before that, dusting and scrubbing and mopping and rinsing for three days from dawn to dusk until every surface shone and reflected my face back at me. They were cleaning again that day, not a very extensive job, but the more surprising thing was the sackfuls of groceries that one of the crew unloaded on the kitchen countertop. With great efficiency, she stocked the fridge and the pantry with enough supplies to last a large family for an entire week.

And that's when it hit me. When I was younger, I never stopped to wonder how the farmhouse always looked ready for us to barge in and unpack, plonk on the sofa, or jump on the beds. There was always fresh, home-cooked food on the dining table. Plenty of chocolates and ice creams for dessert. These were the things we didn't have to think about, because of course Mom and Dad had planned and arranged for everything to be in place long before we drove through the ornate, magical double gates.

This could only mean one thing. After five long years, the Classions were gearing up to put an appearance at the farmhouse once more. I may never know what caused them to stay away from this place for five years. But I knew what was dragging them back here for such an unseasonable visit, whether they realised it or not. A firstborn must have turned fifteen.

As far as I knew, only the twins had turned fifteen in February. And neither was a firstborn.

CHAPTER 15
DÉJÀ VU

The moment I saw Zelda was the moment that exploded into infinity, and also the moment into which the intervening years were compressed. As if no time had passed, yet an eternity had lapsed. So vast was the chasm, yet all the memories of the past flooded it in an instant.

She could have been me. I could have been her. The gulf of five years that separated us in age seemed no longer than five seconds. Twins. Born five years apart.

But that was only in the way she carried herself. Chin up. Head held high. A brazen confidence that brought the room to life, throbbing and pulsing with her youth.

It was a confidence that had flowed through my veins whenever the world around me, the people who mattered to me, acknowledged and appreciated my very existence. I couldn't recall the last time I had felt that way, sure of myself and my place in the world, so long and interminable these past five years had been.

Now that Zelda sauntered into the room, breathless, eager

to see what adventures the farmhouse held for her, forgotten envy clutched at my throat. That should have been me, I thought. Pride of the family. Golden girl. Of course, only metaphorically. My raven-black hair and eyes could never compete with the twins' flax-golden tresses and sea-green eyes. Zelda and Sara took after Mom. They were beautiful people with a feminine grace but an inner strength that took you by surprise if you mistook their vulnerability for weakness.

I had inherited the ruggedness of Dad's side of the family. While the Classion men exuded a raw strength not meant to be trifled with, the women were what you'd call handsome. Strong. Attractive. Certainly not the delicate type.

Growing up, I had been rather the tomboy and my resemblance to Dad and his brother was something I held in great esteem. A special gift that had been bestowed upon me. Something my sisters would never be able to lay claim to.

But now, seeing Zelda saunter in like she owned the world one instant, then twirling her golden locks around her finger like a helpless maiden needing to be rescued the very next instant, triggered in me a long-forgotten feeling of being betrayed.

For Zelda had been the one who had spotted Marcus Ahlgren emerging from the woods that fateful afternoon five years ago, the last time I had splashed about in the creek with my sisters. And Zelda had been the one who had denied all knowledge of his existence when it truly mattered.

And it occurred to me I may not be all that sorry if Zelda were next in line to face the fate that has befallen me. My little sister sometimes shone too bright for her own good. So bright it hurt everyone in her vicinity.

And then there was Sara. There, yet not there. Inconspicuous, as usual. Blending with the shadows. Staying out of the limelight.

Grandma did not accompany the rest of the Classion clan that visited. That was the first indication to me that she was no more. That, and the fact that Sara had been unable to fall asleep on the first night of their visit and had sauntered into Mom and Dad's room, weeping silently, saying how much she missed our grandparents, that the farmhouse brought back memories of them.

I spent that night in bed, trying to grapple with the fact that Dad and Uncle Jensen now constituted the oldest generation of Classions now living in the world.

What was it like to know that everyone who had once looked after you as you had grown up was gone, taking with them all their memories of who you had once been? As a newborn. A toddler. A young little imp, trying to establish who you were amid the din of who everyone else thought you ought to be.

Of course, life wasn't extinguished in the same order in which it manifested. Bonnie and I were proof of that. Outlived by our parents and uncles and aunts. The curse of every firstborn Classion.

Which meant that none of the living members of my parents' generation was a firstborn.

I gasped. The truth had been staring in my face for so long its realisation now landed like a slap across my face and jolted me awake. It gripped my throat in an unknown terror I hadn't even known I could possibly feel after all that had transpired five summers ago. It clutched my heart and twisted it so cruelly that I sat up in bed and cried out in pain, letting out such a loud yelp it woke up the twins in the adjoining room.

"What's wrong with you?" Zelda asked, her voice sleepy and annoyed.

"That wasn't me!" Sara's voice now, soft but with an undercurrent of anger, of defiance.

Moments later, both the girls went back to sleep, having forgotten what had roused them in the first place. But the acrimony between them lingered like a foul odour in the air, a stench rising from years of latent sibling rivalry that no one had wanted to see or acknowledge. Something rotten at the core but could be ignored as long as it was out of sight.

My mind conjured up an image of my old bedroom, not as it was when it had been my haven but what it had become the last time I had entered it. A space being redone to accommodate another. One of the sisters moving out of their shared abode into a place of her own, where she could shut the other one out from all the parts of her life she didn't wish to share. And it occurred to me, not for the first time, that the twins were falling apart and there was nothing anyone could do about it.

But that was the least of my worries, as it turned out to be. Because Dad and Uncle Jensen were now the oldest Classions in the family, neither having succumbed to the family curse when they turned fifteen. Then who had? If neither Dad nor Uncle Jensen was our grandparents' firstborn, then who was?

CHAPTER 16
WAKING UP GHOSTS FROM THE PAST

awn was only just breaking when I reached my parents' downtown home and let myself in using the keys I had nicked from Mom's purse back at the farmhouse.

The ease with which I had startled yet another unsuspecting driver into giving up her car for my use had given me a brief bravado. But now, standing outside the door of my childhood home, keys in hand, as the sky brightened and roused the world around me, I had a sense of déjà vu. Yet again I was about to unearth something I'd never have thought about had I not been a firstborn Classion, cursed to be forgotten by all who loved her.

There was no hesitation this time as I let myself in and ran straight down the hallway, past the living room to the spare room on the ground floor that had once been an ornate sitting room but had been converted into a bedroom for my grandparents' use when they had become too old to navigate stairs and life by themselves with ease.

Heavy drapes smothered the large room, diminishing it in

a frightening manner. I ran to the window and drew back the curtains. The light of the dawn spilled into the room, which almost sighed with relief. The windows covered the entire length of the wall and even in the bleak light of the morning, the room was transformed into a lighter, brighter space, shedding its oppressive heaviness of only a few moments ago.

Dust motes rose from the plush carpet into the air and twirled in the morning light like fragments of my grandparents' souls. The way specks of Grandpa's ashes had escaped the urn and been carried away by the breeze. Fragmented, even in death.

Barring the thin layer of dust that had settled on every visible surface, the room appeared like a museum, an invitation to step into a forgotten era. Pale green wallpaper with a gold-speckled floral motif clung to the tall walls, rising up to meet a leaf-patterned crown moulding that encased the entire room. From the centre of the ceiling hung a chandelier, millions of tiny, delicate pieces of glass twined together to deflect and reflect light from a handful of bulbs that would have looked pretty ordinary on their own but were transformed into objects of beauty themselves, surrounded by all the glamour that honestly belonged in a royal palace.

Every piece of furniture was made of red mahogany, darkened with age. The bed, the doors of the cupboard, the chest of drawers, and even the frame of the oval mirror atop it gleamed brown and burgundy.

The only aberration was Grandpa's wheelchair, a contraption made of metal and synthetic fabric that made for easy cleaning. It was tucked in its usual space between the chest of drawers and the window, the seat sagging a bit from prolonged use, yet ready to wheel its long-time passenger from one room to another.

A deep sorrow rose from within me, and I almost buckled under its unexpected assault. My grandparents were gone. Truly and irrevocably gone.

Even though, or perhaps because, we had lived under the same roof, their presence had never felt fleeting. It had never occurred to me that someday they'd cease to exist. Every longing or desire, dream or regret they had ever held in their lifetime was gone. As if it never was.

I pulled myself together, unwilling to let myself sink into grief or self-pity. I was here on a hunch, and I wanted to follow it, see where it would lead, and what it would reveal to me about the forgotten lives of all the firstborn Classions who had come and vanished like I did.

Grandma must have passed away only recently for the cupboards were still full of my grandparents' belongings.

Long overcoats and flamboyant hats that looked as if they had time-travelled to the present day from a few centuries ago.

The scent of dust mingled with that familiar whiff of dried lavender and another odd smell that I had never been able to place and had assumed was the peculiar odour of the aged and the dying.

Tucked beneath the bottommost shelf were three large cardboard boxes. The floral design gave them a dainty appearance but when I bent to pick them up one at a time and set them on the bed (knowing how much this would have irked Grandma and feeling a trifle relieved that she wasn't around to reprimand me), they were surprisingly heavy and sturdy enough to not buckle under the weight of their contents.

One was full of papers documenting their lives, legit-imising their existence in the eyes of the government and whichever other authority took it upon themselves to demand proof that people were who they claimed to be. Birth certifi-cates. Passports. Immunisation records. Voter cards. Tax documents. No wonder Mom and Dad hadn't been able to bring themselves to go through this endless mess. It was easier to ignore it than rifle through it all.

The second box held memories. Dad's baby book. He had been a tiny baby. 4.9 lb. and 17 in. at birth. Small enough for everyone to worry about and fuss over him but once out of the womb and into this world, he had wasted no time grow-ing. Mashed avocado had been his first solid food. His first word had been 'Mumma'. He had sprouted his first tooth when he was 11 months old. He had taken his first indepen-dent steps shortly after he had turned one.

The entries became sparse and disappeared altogether when Dad was a little older than two years old. Uncle Jensen must have come along then, rendering the filling up of baby books secondary to the actual task of raising them.

There were other memorabilia though. Knitted baby booties and beanie hats with Dad's and Uncle Jensen's names embroidered into them. Digging deeper, I found similar baby paraphernalia bearing my twin sisters' names. I must have had one too, I was certain, and I knew just as well that I'd find nothing belonging to me in this box. Nothing bearing my name or making any reference to my once-upon-a-time exis-tence, or even Bonnie's or any other firstborn Classion's, was to be found anywhere in this world.

Nevertheless, I rifled through the box for clues to the Clas-sions that had disappeared. It was the third box that seemed to hold some promise. It was full of photo albums. The more modern, colour photobooks were stacked on the top, pressing down upon the albums bearing sepia-toned and black-and-white memories preserved between plastic sleeves. So many of these photos had been taken only to commemorate special occasions. Weddings. Birthdays. Holidays.

Dad and I had planned to digitise many old photos over the rest of the summer five years ago, I remembered with a pang.

I perused each image, imagining new faces and beings in them. Wasn't that too much of a gap there between Dad and Uncle Jensen, almost teenagers in this seaside picture taken on a holiday no doubt? Enough space for an older sibling to have once stood and smiled at the photographer, completely unaware of the fate that lay in wait?

I willed the photos to reveal their secrets to me, but they paid no heed. Exasperated, I gathered all the images I had scattered on the bed and dumped them back into the box in no particular order.

The room was aglow and warm with the morning light of the summer sun. If I had been more than quasi-alive, I'd have been starving by then. All I felt was a strange hollow in the pit of my stomach, a gnawing worry that I may have missed something important.

Outside the window, the street had come alive. New parents with prams headed out for their morning runs. Dogs trotted down the street, pulling their owners behind, eager to greet the new day and sniff all its smells. Older children emerged from their houses and set out on their way to wherever it was they were scheduled to spend the day—at school or with friends.

Several years ago, small independent houses had perched across the street from our townhouse. Along had come a builder and razed down every one of them to the ground. Construction workers had brought their loud, enormous vehicles, dug deep holes into the ground, and then proceeded to build townhomes quite similar to ours. I remember sitting with Grandma by the window, watching tall cranes dip and turn, dump trucks making large mountains of stone and gravel, backhoes and excavators scooping and pouring. Grandma knitted scarves and caps without so much as a glance towards her work, and we both used to gawk at all the machinery in fascination, the double-pane windows keeping us fairly removed from the dust and din outside.

The normalcy with which life was unfolding outside made me realise how insignificant we were as individuals. My grandparents were gone. I was gone too, in every sense that should have mattered. My parents and sisters were not here right now.

There was no gaping void to commemorate our absence. No Classion-shaped hole for passers-by to stare and shake their heads at and steer clear of. Like weeds pushing out of cracks in the sidewalk, the world had simply rearranged itself to use up the space we had left behind.

It was a depressing thought. I made my way out of my grandparents' bedroom, past the living room, and went up the stairs to what had once been my bedroom.

The last time I had entered the room five years ago, the space had been in limbo. Suspended in an in-between state, somewhere between shedding what it once was and becoming what it was meant to be. What it had become now. An underwater paradise.

She had gone for teal. Seawater teal. The walls were soaked in this deep underwater colour. Tendrils of golden kelp rose from baseboard to ceiling like young trees with slender trunks standing tall in a forest.

Gone were the custom-made shelves and worktop I had once hunched over, hard at work. The bed that had once graced the centre of the room had been pushed to the wall with the window so that whichever sister of mine had lain claim to this room could fall asleep at night watching the stars in the sky. Only a sheer curtain hung over the window like a rectangle of stardust, rendered whiter and shinier than it was by the dark green surrounding it.

A plain but elegant table and chair made of a bright honey-brown stained wood stood beside the bed. Two rows of book-shelves sat like an awning above the table, holding books arranged by spine colour. An underwater rainbow.

A simple chest of drawers in the light-brown colour keeping to the overall theme of the room was pinned to the wall beside the doorway where I stood, mesmerised. A golden-coloured rug covered most of the floor between the bed and the chest of the drawers.

Curious, I stepped inside the room and looked around, turning slowly, gingerly, almost as if I was wading through water. Strings of fairy lights crisscrossed close to the ceiling from the window to unobtrusive nails on the wall against which the chest of drawers stood.

I sank into the bed and looked out of the window. A tall ash tree in our neighbour's backyard reached out to the sky. Its leaves jiggled in the breeze with not a care in the world this morning. Sunlight made them glow golden.

The house was silent, deep in its own slumber. Occasionally, a vehicle dashed on the street outside with a whoosh, a wave crashing on the shore. Lying on this bed, I could have been anywhere. At the farm. At the beachside. Atop the hills.

Yet I was here, in a place I had once called home, in a room that had once been mine. These walls had been a silent witness to all my secrets and longings, desires and despairs. As much as I had loved this room, I had also yearned for something more, something exciting. Adventures. Acts of daredevilry. Without the company of my sisters to remind me how safe and secure it was to stay ensconced in the cocoon of my family, I had often lain here in this very bed, dreaming of striking out on my own and engaging in great escapades. Had it been my silent prayers answered in such a twisted and bizarre way? Setting me out on an adventure from which there was no return? Thrusting me out of the safeguard of my family in a way that was irreversible?

It was hard to tell which of my sisters had developed a newfound desire for a world other than the here and now. Was it Zelda? The know-it-all. The one who had always been certain of herself. The one who never doubted the world would rearrange itself around her to suit her whims and fancies?

Or was it Sara? The one who had never thought to think for herself. The one who had been content to follow her older sister everywhere like a doting puppy. Had she somehow come to realise she was her own person? And found it in herself to break free, to figure out who she was as an individual and not as a mere appendage of her older doppelgänger?

A door opened and shut. The unexpected sound gave me a start. I sat up straight in the bed, my heart pounding in my chest at an abnormal pace. I had no reason to fear. No one could see or remember me for more than a moment. Yet my body reacted as if it faced imminent danger.

Soft footsteps drew closer and closer. Somebody was coming up the stairs. Without thinking, I hurled myself onto the floor and crawled under the bed, holding my breath and positioning myself so I could peep out without giving myself away.

A pair of legs in jeans and sneakers appeared at the doorway. Whoever it was, paused there, as if looking around, taking in the sights and smells of this room, or checking for intruders, perhaps.

Although my body instinctively wanted to draw back and press against the wall behind me, I held my breath and stayed put, eager to catch a glimpse of whoever had sauntered in.

The person walked into the room and made their way straight to the chest of drawers. They pulled open the top drawer and rummaged through it.

My first thought was that the person seemed to know their way around the house. Was it someone from the family? I would have said one of 'us' but I was no longer part of 'them'. Or someone who knew the family very well? Well enough to have had a spare key to the house? Mom had never taken to leaving a key under a pot or the doormat or with a neighbour. Unless that was yet another characteristic that had changed in these past five years.

It was hard to decipher whether it was a woman or a man. The sneakers were a muted white with streaks of brown on the sides. An old, oft-used pair. The left shoe had a reflective sticker. A strip of rectangle down the centre at the back. No sticker on the right shoe. The jeans fit well but were not snug, as far as I could see. And I could only see up to their knees.

Whoever it was, was now going through the second drawer. There was a certain precision to their method. They conducted a deliberate search, going over each square inch of space slowly and only once.

Whatever it was they were looking for, they found it in the second drawer. I couldn't see what it was, but the search ended. The person pushed the drawer shut and walked out of the room, whistling something tuneless, and pulled the door closed behind them. I stayed under the bed for a few more minutes, straining to hear the sound of the main door being pulled shut. It came, eventually, after what felt like half a day but surely wasn't more than a few minutes. A soft click as a key was turned in the lock. An engine sputtering into life, a few moments later. The sound of a wave crashing on the shore as the vehicle pulled away from the townhouse.

I crawled out from under the bed and sat, leaning against it, on the carpet. Until my racing heart could feel safe enough to slow down.

It occurred to me only then that I could have used my gift of clear sight to determine who the intruder had been, but in seeking to first hide my near-invisible self, I had forgotten all about being able to see the hidden.

When I could stand without my legs threatening to give way under me, I bolted towards the chest of drawers and yanked it open. The top drawer contained an assortment of lingerie belonging to one of my sisters. I felt violated on her behalf. Someone had come and ruffled through her private items without her knowledge or consent, looked through inti-mate details, and walked away casually, likely having found whatever it was they had been looking for. They had known they would find it here. In my sister's room. In her chest of drawers.

I pulled out the second drawer and found a collection of Leuchtturm notebooks. Private journals. My fingers paused over them. They were tantalising. They were stacked in a small shelving unit like a basket within the drawer, spines facing outwards, marked with months and years in neat cursive handwriting on sticker labels.

Even as I debated with myself whether or not to pull out one of the diaries and read them, I looked at the remaining contents of the drawer. Another shelving unit contained an assortment of trinkets. Friendship bracelets, some were beads on strings, some were handwoven. Greeting cards. A tiny blue rabbit that had broken off from the keychain it had once been a part of, three loops of chain still sticking out of the centre of its head.

This was the drawer where the unexpected visitor had found whatever they had been looking for. I pulled out the bottommost drawer. It overflowed with pyjama sets.

Curious, I picked them up and unfolded them one at a time. No unicorns. No rainbows. But lots of glitter. Plenty of quotes on pyjama tops.

Some actually brought a chuckle to my face. *'Money can't buy happiness. That's what shopping is for.'*

Some were angsty. One had the image of a young girl, no older than seven or eight, sitting astride a bike with a grimace on her face and flashing a middle finger at whoever dared to look at her.

I didn't particularly recall my own teenage years, the few that I spent with my family, but I was pretty sure I had rarely crossed the line from independent thinking to outright rebellion.

As I folded the clothes and put them back inside the drawer, it occurred to me that Mom wouldn't have taken kindly to many of these obvious displays of subversion. Whichever of my sisters these belonged to must be caught up in an intense desire for insubordination.

I couldn't leave without knowing who it was. I pulled out one of the journals and flipped it open to the first page. It gave up its secret at last. There was a name. On the top right corner.

The calligraphy was impressively beautiful. The 'S' was all curves with a little crest on its head, like that atop a northern cardinal. Curlicues and flourishes gave the appearance of a river of flowing lines from which emerged a name, bold and clear.

Like the title of a book.

The name of a story.

Sara Classion.

PRIDE BLOOMED in my chest at the sight of my youngest sister's name. Sara. I had been hoping it would be her. I hadn't believed it could be her. Timid Sara. Content to go wherever Zelda went. But life had pulled her in an entirely different direction. And she had made her way here, to a different room. That was a start.

I had a sudden urge to talk to her, lie down with her under the stars and ask her everything about herself. Her dreams and her aspirations. Her desires. Her vision for her life. How had these past five years changed her? Who had she become now?

I tucked the journal back in its place and pushed the drawer shut. I skipped down the stairs and went back into my grandparents' room. The boxes I had rummaged still lay where I had left them on the bed.

There was still one way I knew to bring the past back to life, even if only for my eyes. I carried the three boxes one at a time to the stolen car I had parked right outside the house. Another SUV. But this one was black with pink polka dots all around it. Easily recognisable. Unforgettable. Even so, it remained a non-entity so long as I was in the driver's seat, and I hoped that little shield of protection would stay put until I reached the farmhouse.

CHAPTER 17
SEEING, AND BEING SEEN

Three boxes nestled on the plush carpet beside the bed in my room. An assortment of photographs littered my bed like confetti from a rather raucous party sprinkled all around me.

I had chosen them carefully. A handful few. The ones I guessed held the most secrets. Photographs where there was enough space to accommodate another person or two. Images of landscapes that may have once had people in them, for even I knew photographs were not ubiquitous in the olden days and the beauty of nature was best captured in paintings by professional artists and amateur dabblers alike.

Like the inks of a watercolour crawling back to where they originally belonged, faces and bodies wobbled back into being on the photos, many of these square-shaped black-and-white snapshots no larger than the palm of my hand.

My hands trembled as I reached for the nearest photo that had sprung into life. Three lanky teenagers grinned into the camera, leaning against an old, ginormous car that I recognised as my Grandpas' Ford Anglia. I had never seen the monstrous vehicle myself for it had been sold off at an auction long before I had arrived in this world. He had only had it for a few years before the stroke had left him wheel-chair-bound and unable to ride his beloved car anymore.

I stared at the three people in the photo. Tallest among them all was Dad. A young boy. Not even taller than the roof of the car he leaned against. It was from him that the twins had gotten their infectious grins, an inheritance that Zelda put to much use but one that was wasted on Sara.

Dad was in the centre, having thrown his arms around the shoulders of the other two who flanked him. Uncle Jensen to his right. And a girl to his left. She was not much older than him. The resemblance was unmistakable. The same curve of the mouth. High cheekbones. Faces that shone with happiness.

On the back, in Grandma's neat, tiny writing the following words appeared: Martha, Hugo & Jensen.

Martha. A name, at last.

Hungrily, I gathered the other pictures on my bed and perused them, one at a time. More pictures of Martha appeared alongside Dad and Uncle Jensen. I knew who she was, but I wanted to gather irrefutable proof before I jumped to the foregone conclusion.

I rummaged through the box of documents and found what I was looking for. A birth certificate, testifying that Martha had been born to my grandparents a year before Dad had come along. She had been my Aunt. She had been Dad's and Uncle Jensen's older sister. She had been a firstborn Classion, whose life had been erased from the family's memories.

The truth was so heavy to bear that I leaned back against the bedhead. An eerie chill crept up my spine and neck, spilled over my shoulders and ran down my chest.

I toyed with the idea of drawing up a family tree. What would that be like? Having to add new branches at every level? A missing Aunt. A missing great-uncle or great-aunt. Lives snuffed out before they may have had a chance of birthing new beings to carry on their family name.

With a sweep of my hand, I pushed all the photos and documents from my bed into one of the boxes on the floor right beside the bed, reluctant to put in the effort to sort them.

No amount of organising or chronicling would help make sense of what had been happening to the Classions for generations. No amount of sorting would bring back what was lost forever. Lives innocently claimed.

I slid under the cover and pulled it over to my neck. It was a warm summer evening, I could tell, the way sunshine poured through the windows into my room even though the clock said it was way past dinnertime.

Soft footfalls and voices drifted my way from the corridor outside, signalling the return of the farmhouse guests to their bedrooms for the night.

There.

Zelda's high-pitched squeal.

Mom's and Aunt Melissa's soft tones.

Dad's and Uncle Jensen's voices booming like cannon fire.

Sara's silence.

Bonnie's and my absence.

Aunt Martha's vanishing.

And how many more, who knew?

All the sounds that were and the sounds that weren't but should have been, clashed in my head, clamouring for attention. I pulled the bedcovers over my head to keep them out and for the first time in five years, I slipped into a deep sleep, the kind I had long given up hopes of experiencing ever again.

SOMETHING MOVED beside me under the covers and jolted me into wakefulness. I woke up with a start, pushing the covers away from me and sat bolt upright. Heart in mouth, I turned around to see what had brushed against me.

The moonless night had a deep darkness to it, and it took me a few moments to be able to tell apart the silhouettes from the shadows. But when my eyes grew accustomed to the dark, I found Sara's pale face peering out at me calmly, watching my movements without giving herself away.

So unexpected was her presence that I scooted back and tumbled out of the bed as if I had seen a ghost.

"Sorry if I woke you," Sara whispered. "Zelda's still awake, texting her boyfriends, and I couldn't sleep."

Shock and awe collided in my heart.

"Sara? Can you see me?"

She nodded. "Sure do."

The initial shock gave way to delight. And an emotion I hadn't dared to feel in the longest time. Hope.

I took a few tentative steps and sat on the edge of the bed, afraid to find out that one of us had been dreaming, terrified to have that hope shattered.

"Sara." I whispered her name again. "Is this for real?"

"Uh-huh," she said, nodding again. A yawn escaped her mouth. "I'm so sleepy. Do you mind if I sleep here?"

The years of absence collapsed and dissolved in a rush of affection as if they had never existed. "Of course not, you silly thing," I said, and reached out instinctively to brush her hair away from her face and tuck them behind her ears.

The novel sensation of touch brought tears to my eyes. I had forgotten what it had been like to touch another person, to offer comfort and solace. I hadn't even known I could touch another person. Or was it just Sara? I couldn't even be sure this was not a dream.

I had so many questions to ask my sister, but her eyes were already closed and her body had gone a little slack, the way it used to aeons ago when the twins were younger and I'd read to them at bedtime and they'd fall asleep beside me, leaning into my sides, their shoulders pressing into my waist, their heads drooping over my belly. The way it did the last time they had fallen asleep against me. Five years ago. Out on the farm. Their tongues stained with bright popsicle colours. Watching a summer sunset they had no recollection of the next morning.

MY SISTER WAS GONE when I awoke the next morning. Even before I had opened my eyes, I could sense her absence. An emptiness next to me. I reached out for her with my hand, but I only grasped air. I opened my eyes and confirmed what my body had known, that she was gone as if she had never come.

A sense of despair engulfed me. And I cursed myself for having rendered myself vulnerable by giving in to hope. Hope. That illusion of happiness. That delusion that at some moment in the future, life would be a little more bearable than it was now.

It reminded me of that fateful afternoon when time had stood still and I had set out with a single backpack, determined to walk the countless miles that lay between the farmhouse and our townhome in the city, and the road had kept circling back to the farmhouse.

That was the day I had clung to hope as if it could deliver me from the nightmare that had ensnared me. That was the day I had begun to give up on hope, understanding it was simply another way of wishing reality had been different.

To hope was to wish for what wasn't. To hope was to wish for things and people that weren't. To hope was to acknowledge and admit that what was, wasn't at all what you wanted it to be.

To hope. To pray. All these were merely means by which the desperate turned away from what was staring in their face because their reality was too difficult a burden to bear.

I would have hurled myself into the death spiral of depression had my fingers not brushed against something thin and pointy. A piece of folded paper. I opened it hastily.

Sunset in the fields today?

~S

THERE IT WAS. The curlicues and flourishes in those words were unmistakable. Last night hadn't been a dream. My youngest sister could see me. Touch me. Talk to me.

I had come back to life once more.

CHAPTER 18
NEW HOPE, NEW FEARS

Evening took an eternity to come.

First, the sun just didn't seem to want to rise from behind the horizon although the new day waited with bated breath. Or was it just me? I took to pacing in my room with the unrealistic expectation that it would cause time to hurry up. No such luck!

The room quickly began to feel claustrophobic even though it took me fifteen steps to go from one wall to the opposite. I made my way down the stairs and to the kitchen, eyeing the backdoor that opened to the creek and the willowwacks beyond.

So caught up in my excitement was I that I walked straight past the dining area before realising that the entire family had gathered there for their morning meal. Six heads turned to look up at me in unison.

Dad, looking more and more like Grandpa now.

Mom. More breathtakingly beautiful than ever as though she had found a secret way to grow younger with each passing year.

Uncle Jensen, vying with Dad in a who-resembles-Grandpa-more contest. Aunt Melissa, older, softer, sadder somehow.

Zelda. Impeccably dressed. Surreptitiously clicking away on her mobile phone under the table.

Sara. Looking up at me, expectantly. A small smile on her lips.

Then the moment passed, and everyone's attention drifted back to their toast and eggs, their thoughts and conversations.

Everyone, except Sara that is. She winked at me when no one was looking and turned back to her plate.

That was all the encouragement I needed.

"Surprise!" I shouted, then dashed past the shocked faces with wide eyes and gaping mouths, yanked the backdoor open and ran out onto the grass and up beside the creek, as light and free as laughter.

I wasn't worried about the family I left behind, startled by my momentary presence. They would have forgotten all about me by now. Clearly, only Sara had somehow become aware of my presence in much more than a fleeting, temporary way.

Buoyed by this renewal of a very real and human connection with my sister, I ran and ran, startling the creatures of the wild as I frolicked and whooped and swung from low branches. My legs wouldn't stay still, and my feet didn't want to kiss the ground for longer than a second. On and on I ran without any thought to where or how far I wanted to go.

Eventually though, I grew tired and wanted to rest and sank against the wide, rough trunk of a large ash tree whose branches reached all the way across the creek to the other side, providing the perfect bridge for a pair of squirrels darting from one bank to the other.

The creek was so swollen with all the water gushing down that its shallow bottom was not visible. This summer had witnessed unprecedented rainfall. I gazed at the brown water swirling and twisting its way down to a faraway lake. Something larger than itself, large enough to lose itself into.

The murkiness cleared as the bottom of the creek revealed itself to me. Brown and grey pebbles and rocks worn smooth by the relentless current. Tiny fish racing with the stream. Further beneath, the rich brownness of the soil underneath it all. Worms and other earth creatures perforating the soil, helping it breathe. Roots of the ash tree I was leaning against, reaching out to countless root tendrils of its neighbours. Little fingers seeking each other for comfort. The way I had intertwined my fingers with Sara's last night, wanting to hold on to her even as sleep had lured me back into oblivion.

I turned back to face the farmhouse and sought it out through the dense miles of trees. Everyone was still at the dining table, helping themselves to second and third servings of bacon and toast and eggs. I remembered how our appetites seemed to increase immensely at the farmhouse. *It must be something in the air,* Mom used to say with a smile that meant she was either telling the truth or not. We never found out which.

I inhaled deeply, the thick, muggy, overpowering scent of the woods. And an occasional whiff of lavender. Was it real? Or conjured from a memory? I couldn't tell, but I no longer cared.

Away from the farmhouse, I sought out the clearing atop the hill that overlooked the Ahlgrens' abandoned property.

I hadn't seen Marcus for a long time now. He helped me get through the first year after that fateful summer, after that disastrous visit to my family's downtown home. But as the next cycle of seasons began, he took to wandering off by himself for longer and longer stretches of time. For several weeks, at first. Then for several months at a time. The last time he had swung by the Classion land was well more than two years ago.

And the truth was that I hadn't gone looking for him either, worried that it might remind him there was supposedly another firstborn Classion whose life he was still waiting to claim. Now with all the remaining Classions gathered here at the farmhouse, two fifteen-year-olds among them, I had all the more reason to ensure he didn't turn his attention our way. I shuddered.

But there was no stopping him, was there? Besides, it wasn't as if *he* was intent on prising us away from our families. It was what he was compelled to do. I wondered then how it would have all unfolded had I walked away with him the first time he had asked me to. The night that fell after that fateful sunset, when I had stumbled sleepily after Dad and Uncle Jensen as they carried the twins back into the house from the fields.

As if he had heard my thoughts, Marcus appeared under the oak tree that had kept guard over his ancestor's grave and provided it shade for centuries.

I made my way up to where he was as slowly as I could, wanting to delay the inevitable conversation, preferring instead to have imaginary conversations with him in my head as I went over again and again what to say to him and how to alert him to the latest developments without rekindling his interest in whisking away one of my family.

In the end, all my ruminations did not matter. When I reached the oak tree, Marcus gave me a broad smile, the kind one would give a friend, a comrade with whom one had been in the trenches, seen horrors together. And any doubt I had held in my heart until then about Marcus's intentions dissolved in that instant.

"Where have you been?" We both asked each other at the same time and laughed.

I half-expected him to pave the way for me to begin, ladies' first and all that medieval chivalry crap, but he surprised me.

"I've been trying to find out what, or rather, who is holding me back," he said, looking at me in the eye.

I stiffened. "What did you find?" I asked, not at all certain I even wanted to know the answer.

"Nothing." He shrugged.

I waited but he said no more.

"Does that mean no more Classions will be … will be made to disappear?" I had been about to say 'harmed' but a part of me was intent on being kind and compassionate towards Marcus, no matter what. Whatever he needed to do was not his fault. There were invisible forces at work, and we were mere pawns in this tragedy that had been playing out generation after generation.

But today was different. I had reconnected with Sara and that reunion was nothing short of a miracle. Just as a parent vows to live up to impossible ideals at the sight of their newborn infant, I too was in such high spirits that morning I didn't want anything to mar the beauty of it all.

Marcus shook his head. "I don't know that for certain," he said.

Getting concrete answers out of Marcus was like trying to leach iced tea out of a stone. A nasty thought flitted into my head. Marcus had said he had chosen not to marry or have children so that he'd not be compelled to pass on the burden of his curse to yet another unsuspecting Ahlgren. Looking at him shaking his head, unwilling to present any conjectures, I sent a silent prayer of thanks to the Universe for having spared another human the travesty of marrying someone as commitment-phobic as this man in front of me.

Remembering my resolve to not give in to uncharitable thoughts or behaviour, I shook my head to rid myself of these thoughts and concentrated on the matter at hand. Something else nagged at me. "How would you, I mean, someone like you, go about trying to find answers? Have you been snooping and eavesdropping on people?" I asked.

Marcus raised an eyebrow at me. "What do you take me for?"

I cocked my head and said, "A ghost that can flit in and out of bedrooms unseen, unheard?"

He dipped his head too, mirroring my action, then pointed a finger at his temple and twirled it. "You getting too lonely out there at the farm?"

I grinned at him and shook my head. It took him only a moment to understand what had transpired.

"They're back?" he asked, looking in the direction of the farmhouse.

"Yes!" I nodded excitedly. "After five effing years!"

But Marcus was unable to muster some of his own enthusiasm to match mine. He knitted his brows in worry. "Are your sisters fifteen yet?" he asked.

"Yes," I said, keeping my smile plastered on my face while my stomach flip-flopped. "But there's been another development."

Marcus looked up at me, his face and his entire being tensed as he waited for me to continue.

"Sara can see me," I said in a voice so small I hoped he wouldn't hear me.

But from the way his eyebrows shot up to his hat and his eyes grew wide as if they'd pop out and roll away if he didn't stop straining them thus, I knew he had heard and comprehended what I had just revealed.

"But that's impossible," he gasped. His voice was throaty and raw as if the words had lodged themselves in his throat and he struggled to get them out.

"I think she could see me, and you too, when we paid a visit to my family," I said.

"Five years ago," he whispered, looking out at his ancestral home. Abandoned and in ruins.

"Where were you all this while?"

He shrugged. "Here and there," he said finally. "Making sure I was indeed the last Ahlgren. Trying to reach out to the spirits of my ancestors to seek guidance from them." He turned towards me, spread his hands out and said helplessly, "Because this is me being in limbo. I don't know how to make my way to the other side. There are others like me, trapped here, with no one to guide them to wherever it is that souls go when they depart."

When he said those words, I came to know what kind of a man Marcus Ahlgren was. He sincerely did not wish to inflict this curse of being stuck in limbo on anyone, Ahlgren or Classion. He was a man trapped in a suffering that had nothing to do with him. His only fault was that he was born into the Ahlgren family.

Because at the end of it all, this was the story of our lives, his and mine. Of being stuck in a liminal space, and constantly seeking a way out of it.

I reached out to hug him, forgetting in that instant who he was. I slipped through him and had to put out a hand to steady myself against the tree trunk. My arm went right through the apparition of Marcus Ahlgren who looked as real as you do right now with your flesh and bones all intact but who was made of nothing more than smoke and illusion.

And I pulled myself back recognising that at least I was still lucky enough to be able to touch another human.

"Where did Bonnie go after she vanished from our lives?" I asked, wondering if that would provide some clue. "Was she also trapped for a while like us?"

"Bonnie came with me willingly," he said. "She was the first Classion I had to coax into nonexistence. And I didn't know what to expect."

Remembering the way Marcus had approached me that night, asking me to walk away with him, a complete stranger, I put my hands on my hips and said, feigning disapproval, "Surely you didn't simply put out your hand and say, 'Come away with me'. She'd have thrown you a punch in your gut. Hurt you enough to keep you from coming back."

Marcus grinned. "Too many things wrong with that hypothesis. First, her punch would have gone right through me, leaving me unharmed and her out of balance. Secondly, I approached her rather differently."

"Differently how? Tell me."

"I'll tell you," Marcus said, looking away for an instant, then back at me. "But promise me you will not hold a grudge against me."

I raised an eyebrow, completely intrigued, and so I nodded my head, committing to a promise I knew I'd likely not be able to keep.

"For one thing, I took the time to explain to her the entire saga. And at the end of it, she was pretty convinced that walking away with me was the best choice. The only choice, in fact."

Now I was really annoyed. "Why didn't you employ the same tactic with me then? What was the need to spook me out in the middle of the night? That was the surest way of getting me to refuse," I huffed.

Marcus sighed and said, "Because I wanted to give you the chance to refuse and see if that would somehow break the curse."

I wanted to be mad at Marcus. Heck, I was feeling pretty mad at him right then. Annoyed and irritated with him for the foolish decisions I had made and the consequences of which I had to put up with now. Of course, I was mad at him. How could I not be? But also, how could I stay mad at him? We were in this together, doing what we could within our limited means, with no way of knowing what the consequences of our actions would be.

He was watching me, observing the expressions flitting across my face. Seeing the truth of me. The truth of my inner conflict.

"Thank you, I guess," I said at last, offering my words as

solace even if it wasn't the entire truth. "Even though I'm also mad at you."

"I'm really sorry, Becca," he said softly.

Five years had passed, yet I couldn't let go of the intense longing to go back in time and change everything. The way the faintest whiff of cigarette smoke catches an ex-addict off guard, any suggestion or reminder of the possibility that things could have been different sparked in me a deep desire for all that wasn't and regret for all that I had lost.

Yet, when I turned to Marcus, I found in me the empathy to acknowledge and say, "You were only trying to help." And almost immediately, as if to compensate for the silent rage that had erupted in me against him, I offered, "I'm meeting Sara at the fields this evening. Would you like to join us? Together we may be able to find a way?"

Marcus smiled and nodded eagerly. Delight transformed his face instantly. And I was happy with the choice I had made this time. If there was even the slightest chance to make today and tomorrow worthwhile, I was happy to give up my longings for an unchangeable past and an imaginary future.

CHAPTER 19

A RENDEZVOUS AT
SUNSET

The lavenders were in full bloom and the air was thick with their scent. Above, the sky had turned pale pink, the sun having set several minutes ago, too remote now to set clouds on fire.

My sister had brought a picnic mat and a cooler of popsicles. I had accepted her offer of an ice lolly, a bright blue one, not having the heart to tell her of my loss of appetite and sense of taste. She noticed, though, alerted to the strangeness of my being by the fact that the lolly left no colour on my tongue.

We had spent half an hour together, watching the sun go down. There was so much I wanted to ask her about how life had unfolded for her these past five years, so much I wanted to tell her about all that had happened to me in this time, that I knew not where to begin. Silence had seemed like a good way to start the conversation, and so we both sat there on the mat, licking lollies, and watching the sun. She seemed content, at ease by my side, while I sat rock still, holding every sliver of angst and excitement and nervousness within a tight ball inside me, afraid that the slightest movement would nudge it and cause it to unravel and explode.

Sara reached for a little drawstring bag that sat beside her like an amethyst jewel, such a bright purple hue it had. It clinked as if it held keys or coins or some such metallic item. She pulled a packet of cigarettes and a lighter from the bag, turned the packet upside down and tapped it a few times against her palm, then pulled out a cigarette, stuck it between her lips, and lit it with the practised expertise of someone who had done this often enough.

The long-forgotten maternal instinct swelled within me and I reached out to grab the cancer stick but Sara, anticipating my move, held out an arm and blocked me from getting anywhere close to her cig.

"You're five years too late, sis," Sara said, blowing a plume of smoke rings into the heavens.

"It's not my fault," I cried.

"Never said it was," she smiled, pleased with her own wit.

It only exasperated me. "That doesn't mean you should kill yourself," I said.

"We are always inching closer to death, sis," Sara said, "whether we want to or not."

There was no sarcasm in her voice. Just a resignation. A silent acceptance of the reality of life and all its vagaries. Sara had always been the observant one in our family.

"Five years I leave you to your devices and you've begun spouting wisdom," I said to her and tapped her on the arm lightly.

She grinned, then stretched out her legs and lay down on one side, turning towards me so one arm was still free to bring the cigarette to her lips and away as she pleased. Her eyes had grown greener since the last time I'd seen them. Green with flecks of golden honey, like the green of newborn leaves in springtime. Her hair fell to her shoulders in lazy waves. She had little makeup on. Only the sheen of a pink lip gloss outlined her lips immaculately, although I suspected she undertook this effort to hide how her smoking habit was slowly charring her lips an unhealthy black.

"I was always the wise one, Becca," she said with a sigh. "You're the one who's noticing it five years too late."

"You were always content for Zelda to stand in the lime-light," I said, wanting to understand what had prompted the smarter, sassier of the twins to hide her true nature.

Sara shrugged. "You all thought I was the more timid one. I didn't see any reason to disabuse you all of that notion. I always knew who I was. And that was enough, as far as I was concerned."

What could I say to that? It was true. Raising three kids had been hard enough for Mom and Dad. Looking after two younger sisters had proven easy for me when one was simply willing to go with what the other said or did, no questions asked. Sara had always been the quiet one, the obedient one, the one who hardly fussed. The easy child. Easy for Zelda. Easy for Mom. Easy for me. But hardly easy for her own self. And who could find fault with the very ingenious way she had come up with to cope with the situation? Simply allowing everyone to believe the stories they had concocted about themselves, about her and Zelda, while she stood apart from it all in her own mind, certain of what she thought and felt.

"Do you remember the first time we camped out in the backyard?" she asked.

"We did?"

"Yes. It was only that one night though."

"When was it?"

"On your seventh birthday."

I searched in my mind, but no suitable memory offered itself. I shook my head. "You must have been only two years old then. How on earth do you even remember it?"

"Because of what happened," Sara said. She pulled herself up, rummaged in her drawstring bag, produced an ashtray from it and flicked the burnt, lopsided end of the cigarette into it.

"What happened?"

"It was the first time I saw a ghost," she said.

"A what?" I shouted, unable to stop the fear hurtling out of me.

"A ghost," Sara repeated, appearing nonchalant. I couldn't tell if this was the impression she wanted to convey or if this bizarre calmness was something she truly felt.

"You poor thing," I whispered. "You must have been terrified."

She dragged on her cigarette and shook her head. "Actually, no. I hadn't learnt by then that I was supposed to be scared of ghosts. I guess it helped to get to know them at such a young age, long before I had had the opportunities to form biases and become prejudiced against them."

When I couldn't come up with a suitable response, she continued. "I have seen them all around us ever since."

She looked around and I followed her gaze with a shiver. Stars winked at us through a periwinkle blue sky. There was still enough light to see by, but it was on the verge of disappearing. Even though I had grown accustomed to Marcus's presence and to living like a ghost myself, I couldn't imagine a two-year-old being exposed to phenomena even grown-ups had a hard time believing, let alone accepting.

I scanned the fields for Marcus, but he wasn't here yet. Or even if he was, he was staying away and for that I was grateful because there was so much more I wanted to talk to Sara about that I couldn't bring myself to wait for another such occasion that may or may not present itself.

"Did you tell anyone?" I asked her.

Sara didn't answer immediately. She sat staring in the distance for a few moments, dragging on her cigarette and letting the smoke out in fancy rings that wobbled and shivered as they went up before crumbling and disappearing completely.

"I did," she said at last. "Only once, though. It was a big mistake, and I swore I'd never do it again."

A light breeze picked up and tossed her wavy hair onto her face. A stray strand landed on the burning end of the cigarette and sizzled as it burnt. I scooted closer to her, then pulled one of the little clips I had used to keep my hair in place and slid it over her scalp. It was a gesture of love and she let me offer it to her, neither bitter at such a belated offering nor regretful that it hadn't come sooner.

Her revelation explained a lot. It explained why she had chosen to hide in Zelda's shadows, why she had been content with the lack of attention. Not being under the scrutiny of others had made it easier for her to hold on to her own truths and explore them, whether others believed in them or not. I admired my sister for her courage. For knowing, even at that young age, what truly mattered and what didn't.

"I saw Bonnie once, you know," she said.

Startled, I stopped caressing her hair and shuffled to sit

right beside her so I could see her as she spoke. My sister had proven to be full of surprises since last evening.

"You remember Bonnie?" I asked, my voice a fearful croak.

"Of course, I do. She and you were thick as thieves. It was only after she disappeared that you turned your attention towards Zelda and me."

"No way!" I refuted her automatically and in the same breath I knew I was wrong. As far as I remembered, I was always doting on my younger sisters, helping Mom look after them ever since they were born. But of course, that was only the story I had been telling myself ever since all traces of Bonnie's existence had been wiped out of our lives. That was the story that first sprang to mind whenever I thought of home, of Mom, of my sisters.

But other memories began to form more vivid pictures in my head. The memory of a recollection.

The story of Bonnie and Becca. Both children of summer. Bonnie with the purple hair that cascaded like a waterfall down to her knees. Uncle Jensen and Dad asking Bonnie and me to stand against the kitchen doorway, marking our heights in purple and pink. Bonnie reappearing in all the photos she had vanished from. As if her images had been printed in disappearing ink and reappeared only if you knew how to bring them back.

Even then it had occurred to me how much more I had shared with Bonnie than with the twins.

Grief and loss roared anew inside of me. Like magma deep within the core of the earth. "How do you know all this?" I snapped at Sara.

"Because I see, Becca," she snapped back. "I see and I remember. I don't forget like the rest of you do."

"You make it sound like we have a choice," I yelled back.

"Thank your lucky stars you don't. Because you're not the one walking around seeing the ghosts of the dead and hearing their plaintive cries, their desperate pleas for release from limbo. You're not the one trying to look away when a spirit gets too close to you, hoping that just because you can see them you can somehow liberate them. You're not the one trying to hide your true self from everyone else just so that they are not inconvenienced."

The pain in her voice was palpable and I knew I ought to soothe her, placate her, or at least keep my mouth from spewing the wrong words.

But that was the thing about family reunions. Along with a gush of affection came an almost indisputable licence to hate the other person, even if only momentarily, to hold them accountable for everything that may have gone wrong in your life in the time you spent with them.

And so, instead of comforting Sara, I looked at her with all the coldness I could muster, pointed a finger at her and said, "And you, Sara, you should thank your own lucky stars that you weren't the one to disappear. Because you still have a life you can live. So quit moaning and make of it what you will. I don't even have that option anymore."

"Ha!" Sara spat. "I wish I had been the one to disappear. I wish I had been the one to get away from that miserable lot." She jerked her head towards the farmhouse.

"You don't mean that," I said.

Sara looked at me for a few moments, breathing hard, the fight going out of her slowly. In the dark of the night, her irises gleamed a soft white like a seagull's feathers. The air between us was hot, incensed, as if our combined angst had set it on fire.

"You know better than to say that, Becca," Sara said. "I've lived in Zelda's shadow all my life. It is perfectly valid for me to want to get out of that."

I should have known better. The fight never went out of Sara. She was not one for angry outbursts and pugnacious debates, notwithstanding this argument that sat like a heavy boulder between us, separating us. Hers was a quiet aggression, the kind that was rarely on display, but when it reared its head, she struck fast and hard.

I stared at her in awe. Who was this young woman sitting in front of me? She was nothing like the timid girl I remembered from all those years ago. Regret unfurled in my chest for all the times I saw Sara and Zelda only through the lenses of the stories I had made up about them. Character sketches I had drawn for them in my head. Sara, the quiet one. Zelda, the boisterous one. Sara, the obedient follower. Zelda, the confident leader.

But no one truly was what we thought they were. We simply didn't have the capacity to see other people for who they truly were, so foggy our lenses of worldview had become because of our own beliefs and fears, because of the fantasies we spun in our heads as we railed against our realities.

"I am sorry," I said, bowing my head, hoping those overused, clichéd words would somehow still manage to convey how truly regretful I felt.

Sara, bless her heart, pulled me into a hug and kissed me on the top of my head. "It is who we are, sis," she said softly into my hair. "We become our stories."

CHAPTER 20
CONVERSATIONS AT TWILIGHT

In a departure from routine, my family stayed at the farmhouse for two weeks that summer as if to compensate for not having put in an appearance for five years.

When I was younger and still living with them, still a very memorable part of the family, our farmhouse visits usually lasted only for three days or so, four at most. But we came here almost every other weekend.

Their extended stay this year was a delightful surprise because after our first evening of catch-up, which lasted until the sun came up, Sara and I fell into a routine of meeting each other in the fields every evening. No one bothered us here. Zelda rarely came out of her room in her spare time, let alone the farmhouse, when she wasn't helping at the gift shop. She was living her life out on her phone, Sara informed me, juggling three boyfriends in one go in her virtual life, while also eyeing a cute high school kid who was working at the gift shop that summer.

Mom, Dad, Uncle Jensen, and Aunt Melissa, busied themselves with overseeing the operations of the farm, assigning tasks to farmhands, replenishing supplies at the gift shop, and scheduling events for visitors. One or more of them occasionally went back to the city to oversee the family business there, not wanting to be away from any of their other ventures for too long at a stretch.

No matter what went on in the fields during the day, come sunset time it was ours. No other soul in sight. As far as I could see, at least. If Sara saw any ghosts drifting along, stopping to smell the lavender blooms, she made no mention of it.

"I saw Bonnie once, you know," she said, in an eerie repetition of the words she had used that first evening when the conversation had devolved into an argument of who had it worse: the one who had to disappear but wanted to be seen, or the one who could see everything and was desperate to unsee it all.

This time, I knew better than to head down that path. And I understood what Sara meant. She had seen Bonnie after her disappearance.

"What had she become?" I asked.

"Like a stem of lavender," Sara said, dreamily.

I didn't understand. "What do you mean?"

Sara raised a finger and pointed to the long rows of lavender plants that began a few feet away from where we sat. "She was drifting there," she said. "Hovering beside that row. I couldn't tell at first. Her purple hair had become translucent like the rest of her, and she blended in with the plants."

"When was this?" I asked.

"Last summer," Sara said. "Zelda, you and I were coming back from the gift shop. I stopped to smell the flowers like I always did."

"We used to tease you about that. About not having had enough of the scent of lavender."

I also remembered how Zelda was always the one running straight through the fields, making her way to the farmhouse or the gift shop, while Sara tended to linger behind, running for a bit to keep up with Zelda, but often stopping by a plant to smell or caress it or simply to admire the way its beautiful flowers curled. Not for the first time did I feel a pang of regret for my sister who had seen and known so much but had no one to unburden herself to.

"Not you." Sara shook her head. "You were always kind to me. Only Zelda. The flowers smell different than all the fancy trinkets in the gift shop do."

And it warmed my heart to hear her say that. Memory was a funny thing. Mine often reminded me of everything that had gone wrong, all that I could have done better, the myriad ways in which I tried and failed or didn't try at all. But if I let those stories slide, I could see glimpses of all my good deeds, the kind things I said or did, the gestures of love I showed, the care and affection I expressed towards both my sisters in equal measure.

"Is that when you saw Bonnie?" I asked.

"Yes," Sara said. She reached for a cigarette, and I had to wait until she lit it up and took the first drag, a long, slow, deliberate drag. The strong scent of clove hit the back of my throat, a spicy contrast to the sweet fragrance of lavender. The rings of smoke she so expertly crafted wafted away like ghosts.

"This is what she looked like," Sara said, pointing towards the translucent wisps of smoke that curved up and away from her cig. "Translucent. Wispy. Like a reflection in a pond, easily disturbed by the slightest ripple."

"Did she know you could see her?"

A smile appeared on Sara's face at the memory. "She gave a start at first. Imagine that! A ghost being spooked by a human. But she hadn't been a ghost for long by then. She had disappeared only the previous night."

Another draw from her cigarette. Yet another bunch of smoke-ring ghosts huffing and disappearing around us.

"She jumped a few feet into the air and stayed there, hovering, looking down on me. And then she smiled."

I imagined Bonnie giving a sad smile, but something was wrong with that picture in my head. Bonnie had been such a lover of challenge that despair or sadness didn't dare invade her space. Sara confirmed my suspicions.

"Not smiled, she actually grinned," Sara said. "That cheeky grin of hers which meant that she was up to no good."

"I remember that," I said, smiling, as Bonnie the daredevil grinned in my mind. "What happened then?" I asked, eager. It occurred to me that whatever happened to Bonnie was likely what would happen to me too. And I was curious to know. The likelihood that I might find Bonnie at the end of this journey, this period of waiting, made me giddy with excitement. Or perhaps that was the effect of the smoke Sara was sending my way in copious amounts.

"She waved to me. Then she looked around," Sara said, choosing to demonstrate this with actions, "puckered her lips into an O, making her eyes just as wide, and put a finger on her lips. And then she winked at me. As if she were sharing a big secret with me. A secret no one else could know."

Sara looked comical now, her green eyes so wide as if

they'd pop out, her long forefinger on her glossy lips, telling a spooky story with a dramatic flair that matched Bonnie's.

"And poof!" Sara said with a sudden movement of her hands, startling me. "She was gone. Off on some grand adventure all by herself."

I almost chided my sister for startling me, but it also occurred to me that the sudden disappearance of Bonnie would have alarmed ten-year-old Sara in precisely the same manner. Instead, I said, "You've developed a flair for drama."

Sara winked at me. "Another one of my hidden talents." And she went back to dragging on her cigarette as if all the answers to every mystery of life lay in those ephemeral rings of smoke she let out with every breath, slipping small slivers of her soul into them to be dispersed into the aether.

I turned my thoughts to Bonnie. If what Sara said was right, Bonnie had died the night she had been erased from our memories. She had lingered about as a ghost for barely a day before vanishing.

"Did you ever see Bonnie again?" I asked.

She shook her head. "She's no longer a ghost. I didn't sense her after that day."

"What do you mean?"

"I can only see spirits when they are in the vicinity. But even if they are someplace else and I can't see them, I can sense their presence in our realm. But when they move on, I can sense they're gone. It's difficult to explain. But I think you understand."

I did, so I nodded. A thousand questions whirred in my mind.

"Do you know where these spirits go?"

Sara shook her head. "No. And frankly, I don't want to

know either. What if there's only a deep, dark, bottomless pit of hell at the end of all this? I'd much rather not know."

She had a point. Another question pressed itself to the forefront of my mind. "Sara, Bonnie lingered as a ghost not even for a day after her disappearance. Then why am I still around? Is it because she went voluntarily? That's what Marcus said."

"Marcus? That cowboy ghost you've been hanging around with?"

I laughed. The only cowboys I had met in my brief lifetime were the ones I had read about in romance novels. Yet, despite his wide-brimmed hat and riding boots, I had never once looked at Marcus as a cowboy. Whether it was because he had had nothing to do with herding cattle or riding horses in his life—he had worked at a malt distillery in the city, coming up with different types of expensive concoctions to keep the wealthy intoxicated—or whether it was because that quin-tessential element of romance had been completely absent from our association, I couldn't tell.

Perhaps, it was because cowboys were supposed to be young and carefree, from what I had read. And Marcus was neither. Five summers ago, he had been more than twice as old as I. And we were in a situation too grave to accommodate fun and frolic. I could never look at Marcus without thinking of the weight of our ancestors' angst pressing down upon both of us.

"The one and only," I replied. "I take it you can see him too."

"Yes," Sara said, craning her neck to look in the distance behind me. "He's been hovering on the edge of the woods since yesterday. Would you like me to call him?"

Without waiting for my answer, Sara raised her arm and waved, then made a gesture of beckoning with her hand. I snapped my head around but saw no one for a moment.

And then Marcus stepped out of a thin, invisible veil of air, as if he had just been on the other side of it all this while.

"Hey," I said, stifling a laugh as I tried to picture him on the cover of a romance novel. Astride a horse. Tipping his head. A sly smile on his lips. The image was so odd it was comical.

Marcus tipped his hat at us and settled himself down a few feet away from us on the grass.

No introductions were necessary, but I went with the formalities anyway. We were an odd trio. A ghost, a near-ghost, and a ghost seer. Because I still couldn't bring myself to believe that I was the spirit of Becca, almost dead and gone. After my transformation, I had slowly come to accept my state of quasi-existence, and now I was just as reluctant to give that story up completely.

But seeing Marcus and Sara here reminded me of the other times we three had been together in the same spot. The most heart-breaking time was when I had made my way to the city to see my family for the first time since my erasure from their lives. When Zelda had gotten into the car of their friend, Beth, and for a split second, Sara had looked at me and then at Marcus and shrugged briefly. Of course, she had seen us then. I asked her about it, and she admitted as much.

But there was another time, the very first time I had seen Marcus, when his spirit had come tumbling through the woods. When the girls and I had been splashing about in the creek.

I had seen him.

And so had one of the twins.

Who's that? one of them had shouted.

And I had assumed it was Zelda. The older twin. Always eager to make her presence known, desperate to make somebody's, anybody's, acquaintance. But unless Zelda had the ability to see ghosts, she couldn't have been the one calling out, demanding to know more about the stranger who had appeared in our midst.

I turned to Sara. My lack of comprehension must have been evident on my face for she took one look at me and said, "You look like you've seen a ghost." And then she laughed and hooted at her own wit. Whatever she was smoking was not simply tobacco, I was convinced.

"That day, the first time I saw Marcus—" I began.

Sara's face shifted into a more sombre expression. She knew what I was talking about. "It was me," she said, before I even had a chance to pose my question. "I knew he was a ghost at first sight but then you noticed him too. And I thought I must have been mistaken."

"That's why you asked who it was," I said.

She nodded.

"That explains a lot," I said, thinking of how vehemently Sara had come to her sister's defence the morning of the big quarrel on the upstairs landing at the farmhouse.

If Zelda says there was no one in the woods, then that's all we need to believe. That's what Sara had said, sealing the dispute once and for all. And she had marched off into the twins' room with Mom and Zelda in tow. And with the same momentum, they had all made their way out of the farmhouse, leaving me behind.

One word from Sara could have changed all that. A single admission of the man we had seen in the woods. Heck! She need not even have labelled him as a ghost. But she chose not to stand up for me that day and let everyone believe I had lost my mind.

I wanted to yell at her but that would have served no purpose. That big ball of angst that had grown and sat between Sara and me the other day like a rock that wouldn't budge reappeared now, at least from my perspective.

"I was scared," Sara said, as if reading my thoughts. She placed a hand on my arm. "I was only ten."

I had forgotten what an astute observer my sister was. My body throbbed with all the emotions I felt, and she sensed them all even if I lent them no words.

And I had also forgotten she had only been a child five years ago. A child who had taken to concealing the truth for the sake of survival. I nodded, reluctantly acknowledging the futility of my despair while also recognising this was the only way our lives and deaths could have unfolded. Some petty part of me wanted to cling to the belief that things could have been different. But the truth was this: whether or not Sara had admitted to seeing Marcus in the woods, the curse of the Ahlgrens would have still come to fruition and separated me from my family one way or the other.

Shaking my head to rid myself of these thoughts, I decided to look ahead. Sara had seen Bonnie leave this realm to go to another, so she might know something that could help Marcus with his onward journey.

"We were talking about Bonnie before you came," I said to Marcus. "Sara saw her spirit move on."

Marcus's interest was piqued. He turned to Sara, his eyes pleading for knowledge, and said, "I've been trying to find my way out of here, but all my efforts have come to nothing. Anything you know, might help."

Sara turned towards the horizon, which appeared bruised. A dark patch of purple-grey pressed down upon a layer of incandescent pink-orange that cleaved the sky into two. One part still sun-kissed. The other out of its shiny reach.

"I must have been five or so," she said, looking into the distance to aid with her recollection. "There was a ghost in our home in the city."

I stiffened. Our lovely, cosy house was the last place I'd have expected to be haunted.

"It was the spirit of a young woman. Somehow related to the previous owner of our home. She used to keep saying, *I need to know the truth. I need to know the truth.* I didn't know what she meant at the time." Sara then turned to me and said, "Do you remember that time when they started to tear down the old houses across the street to build swanky new townhomes?"

I remembered. I had thought about it only a few days ago when I had stood at the window in my grandparents' room and looked out at the townhomes across the street. Built on the graveyards of older homes a decade ago. Another memory released itself alongside.

A sudden recollection seized me. "That's where they found the bones of a baby in the foundation," I said. A small shudder seized my body.

"Exactly!" Sara snapped her fingers.

"But they never found out who the child was. The investigations were inconclusive."

"Turns out it was the child of the ghost woman," Sara said. "Her spirit was tethered to this realm until she could discover the truth about her infant. The man who owned our town-home before we did, had an insatiable appetite for the company of young females. But when they brought little ones into this world, seeded by him, he had the babies disposed of." Sara made a gesture of slitting her throat with a finger.

"What a monster! Why didn't the mothers do anything about it?"

"They were simply told their children were stillborn."

"What happened to the spirit after this discovery?" Marcus asked. He had a pained expression on his face.

"The truth set her free," Sara said. "She left our world and I've never seen her since."

"Does that mean Becca and I have some truths to learn? Is that why we're still here?"

Sara shrugged. "I suppose so."

"Have you seen this happen to any other ghosts?" I asked.

"Yeah, Grandma and Grandpa." Sara's reply was instantaneous.

"What?"

"Yeah. When Grandpa died, he didn't linger for long. He spent a day and a half drifting all around the house. I suspected he was getting used to his newfound mobility after having been wheelchair-bound for so long. And then he was gone."

"Did he say anything to you?"

"I pretended I couldn't see him. I already told you, I don't like responding to these spirits. The instant they realise I can discern them, they stick to me like leeches, hoping I can help them in some way. I don't want to get caught up in all that."

If Sara's remark made Marcus uncomfortable, he did a very good job of keeping a poker face.

"What about Grandma?" I asked.

"She hovered about for a month or so," Sara said with a sigh. "She didn't bother me, but she hung around Mom a lot."

"Mom?" I yelled in surprise. "What does Mom have to do with all this?"

"I don't know," Sara whined and reached for another cigarette. Her third? Or fourth? I had lost count.

This was probably the longest she had talked about ghosts and spirits. This was probably the only time she had talked about them at such length, and it must have been exhausting. It must have taken a lot out of her. Marcus must have understood this too, for he sat silently, patiently, time not a foe to be conquered.

I leaned back and looked up at the stars. There were so many of them, each so small and seemingly inconsequential. Their beauty lay in their collective twinkling. Each like a small sparkly nailhead, keeping the darkness pinned to the skies as much as they could, and not always succeeding.

The fields and the woods around us were dark. Even the creek was silent. Night creatures occasionally shrieked and hissed, but we had long grown accustomed to their presence. Theirs was not a sound that drew attention. It was a melody that blended into the dark.

The house was a darker-than-dark silhouette. Ghostly light quivered behind a lone window. Someone watching the tele or Netflix on their laptop to escape a sleepless night.

The night was warm and our breaths did not mist in the air. But smoke rings drifted heavenwards like trembling wraiths. And not for the first time did I imagine little fragments of Sara's soul permeating the air around us.

The Sara of five years ago could have been coaxed into

doing my bidding, but the one sitting here, with Marcus and me, smoking a cigarette, blowing clove-scented rings into the air, making her own ghosts, had become a force to be reckoned with. *What other terrors have haunted you all these years, my dear sister,* I wondered but dared not ask.

Instead I turned to Marcus and asked, "Do spirits try to take over a human body?"

Marcus shook his head doubtfully and said, "I've never tried. Never had the urge to. Even if it were possible, I wouldn't know how to go about it."

"They don't," Sara said. "It's not what they want, anyway. They don't want to possess people and make them do stuff against their will. They only want to find out whatever it was that continues to haunt them even after death."

We relapsed into silence. Sara stubbed out her cigarette and promptly reached for another one. It felt as if we had run out of things to talk about.

"We leave in a few days," Sara said.

"Oh!" That was all I could say. Her declaration came as a surprise. I had gotten so used to hanging out with her every evening this past fortnight that I had almost forgotten these rendezvous would have to come to an end, sooner or later.

"School begins in a fortnight," she said simply.

It took me a moment to wrap my head around the idea of school. High school. I had only spent a year in high school before my life had spiralled in an entirely different direction. Sara would soon begin her second year of high school, a rite of passage I had completely bypassed. We had spent all these days talking about spirits and ghosts, and now I wanted to know all about her real life, the one filled with real people and situations. I wanted to know it all. The excitement. The drama. The heartbreak. Everything.

"What's school like?" I asked. "Is there someone you like?"

A faint blush crept up Sara's neck, and it occurred to me that I should not have been able to see it in the dark. But somehow, in these past few days, my night vision had been getting clearer and clearer. Just as I could see through and within anything, I was also beginning to see more clearly without the aid of light, natural or otherwise.

"There is someone, yes," she whispered, almost afraid to spill the beans.

I wanted to know more but by now I had learnt that the best way to coax something out of Sara was to let her reveal her truths at her own pace.

As if she had heard my thoughts, she suddenly looked up at me and said, "You probably remember her. Beth!"

"Beth? Lisbeth? I thought you hated her!" Beth of the chauffeur-driven Audi. Beth who had air-kissed Zelda and dragged her into the car, the two forming an impenetrable shell of friendship, while Sara stood on one side like a third wheel. "And wasn't she very thick with Zelda?"

Sara threw her head back and laughed. "I knew you'd remember her," she said when she finally managed to catch her breath. "After you disappeared, Zelda and I started to drift apart. Not that there was much to hold us together in the first place."

I winced inwardly at yet another reminder of how we had been guilty of slotting Sara and Zelda together, not even pausing to consider that the younger twin might have had a mind of her own.

"Is that why you moved into my room?" I asked.

Zelda's eyes lit up. "You saw that? Do you like how I've done it up?"

I smiled, remembering how I had felt entirely at home in my old room, now Sara's haven. The underwater ambience. The bed by the window under the stars. The fairy lights. "It is truly gorgeous."

"It also helped me feel closer to you," she said.

I reached out and squeezed her arm. It is one thing to grow up a lone child, and quite another to have siblings with whom you couldn't connect. Loneliness hurts more when you have company and you're more alone than when you're all by yourself.

Sara's voice drowned out my thoughts. "Anyway, that's when we, rather Zelda, started to hang out more with Beth," she was saying. "I was only ever with them when Beth's chauffeur drove us to school or camp and back."

"Then how come Beth ends up with you and not Zelda?"

"They both fell for the same guy in our class, can you believe that? But he had eyes only for Zelda. The two had a falling out. Enter Sara. A shoulder to cry on. Friend-turned-girlfriend."

I wanted to chide Sara for getting into a relationship with Beth when she was clearly on the rebound. But there was a challenge in Sara's eyes, a defiance in the way she thrust her chin at me, quite remarkably like Bonnie used to, daring me to comment on her unwise decision. And I had learnt she was made of sterner stuff than anybody had ever given her credit for. So I let this one slide.

"You girls and your teenage dramas," I said, rolling my eyes.

"It's fun," she laughed. "You ought to swing by someday

and see for yourself. Zelda's got three guys wrapped around her little finger, and neither one of them has any inkling about the other two."

I shook my head, laughing. I had always wondered what high school would turn my sisters into and I wasn't sure then if Sara's revelations took me by surprise or whether I had grown accustomed to expecting the unexpected. If our lives could change at any instant, how much does our past truly influence our present?

"So, what next?" Sara piped up again. "What's going to happen to you two?"

Marcus and I shook our heads. Both of us were clueless. We had no idea why we were still lingering in this realm. There were no more firstborn Classions for Marcus to guide away from their lives. And as far as I knew, there had been no other secret or mystery in my past that needed to be unravelled before I could depart from this world once and for all. The curse of the Ahlgrens was enough of a secret from the past for a lifetime, as far as I was concerned.

I remembered that I hadn't met Marcus after my last visit downtown, so I brought him up to speed on what I had discovered about my aunt, Martha. Even Sara had been able to see her in the photos I had brought back to the farmhouse.

Still, we were no closer to deciphering what we were waiting for.

"Zelda's firstborn?" Sara suggested.

Marcus moaned. "Who knows how long that's gonna take? I don't want to hang around waiting for that to happen."

"Or you could kill Zelda and me, end the Classion line right here, right now. End of story," Sara said, her eyes glinting in the dark.

"Surely you don't mean that," I gasped.

"Of course, I don't," she laughed. "But you know, it's not really a bad idea." She turned to Marcus and taunted, "Isn't that what your ancestor wanted? To rid the world of Classions once and for all?"

Marcus thought for a moment, then said easily, "I think she wanted them to live and suffer. Death would have been a very easy way out for them."

CHAPTER 21

FAMILY TREE WITH NO BROKEN BRANCHES

Not knowing how much longer my sister would be around to assist us in our inquiries, Marcus, Sara, and I drew up a plan for investigation. Sara pinned large sheets of paper to the walls of my bedroom at the farmhouse. My bedroom that Sara had long declared was her room to the rest of the family. After that first night when she had climbed into my bed and fallen asleep beside me, Sara had moved all her stuff to this room we now shared.

Left to our own devices, we boldly transformed this space into an investigation room of sorts. Sara accompanied Dad on one of his trips downtown and came back with reams of paper and an assortment of stationery supplies. Pens, stapler and pins, tape, markers. Everything we needed to take our thoughts and ideas out of our heads and put them down on paper, so we could step back and find what had been eluding us all this while.

Of course, Sara was the only one who could put pen to paper with the desired consequence. I tried to doodle along one corner, but the lines disappeared faster than the ink could dry. Marcus couldn't even lift a pen. This was the kind of stuff that made me pause and acknowledge that I hadn't become as insubstantial as a ghost. Not yet, at least. There was still work to be done, and it appeared I wouldn't dissolve into the aether until I had completed it.

Sara drew a family tree of the Classions, first writing down the names of the relatives we knew and then adding in the names of the forgotten ones, the ones whisked away from existence because of a curse.

A small sense of satisfaction settled upon my heart as we wrote Martha beside my father and Uncle Jensen, and placed Bonnie under Uncle Jensen and Aunt Melissa. Order restored. Even if only somewhat.

It was thrilling, to say the least. As if we were writing down clues on the board and trying to coax some answers out of it. Sara wrote in a beautiful cursive hand, adding tiny motifs and designs at appropriate places, so the entire wall looked as if it had been plastered with custom wallpaper. A dedication to the Classion family.

She even added Dad's and Mom's signatures under their names, exhibiting the skill of a practised forger.

H. R. Classion, for Dad. Hugo Renfrew Classion, a name that sounded as formidable as the man himself.

And *H. R. Lange*, for Mom. Heather Rainier Lange. Although she had adopted the Classion family name, she had not changed her signature. "Then I'd have had to start signing as H. R. Classion too." Mom had once exclaimed. "Imagine all the confusion *that* would have led to!"

Sara's imitation was excellent. Funny how the Classion

siblings had been endowed with an easy knack for criminal pursuit.

We stared at the family tree but nothing popped out at us the first couple of days.

"Should we draw an Ahlgren family tree?" Sara suggested.

We turned to look at Marcus. He thought for a few moments, then shook his head. "It would take me a very long time to gather all the details. And I wouldn't even know where to begin. We don't have records painstakingly drawn up and preserved like yours," he said, gesturing towards the papers and photographs and albums and trinkets that crowded atop the bed and the chest of drawers in the room.

"It was your great grandfather who moved away from the farm to the city, wasn't it?" I asked, recollecting what Marcus had shared with me about his ancestors.

He nodded.

"Did anyone stay back at the farm then?" I asked.

"Not that I know of," he said. "He had two sisters who sailed away to other continents after marriage. We don't even know where their families are, whether they had any children in the first place. You reckon something like this must be going on between Ahlgrens and Classions in other parts of the world too?"

"I don't know," I said.

"Not that we would have heard about it had any such thing transpired," Sara said. "No one would have remembered anything anyway."

That was what made the entire endeavour so arduous. The ones who knew the truth, or had known it once upon a time, no longer remembered it.

We hung around in silence for a while. Marcus hovered by

the window, his feet a few inches above the ground. I hadn't noticed this before. He had lost his shadow long back, and even though he appeared to be made of flesh and bones, he was an apparition that couldn't be touched. Now it was as if even gravity was beginning to lose its hold on him. I was beside the bed where I tried to surreptitiously jump into the air and see if I could stay afloat. No such luck.

"You're not *dead* dead yet," Sara smirked.

"Why not? I still don't get it."

"Because you were taken before your time," she explained.

"That's right," Marcus said, and I turned around to look at him. "If I wasn't bound by the spell to erase your life, you'd have lived. All these years."

"For how long?" I asked.

"Until whenever you were destined to die," he said.

"But Bonnie died," Sara said, voicing my own thoughts. "Right after she disappeared."

"Which means curse or no curse, she would have died that night," Marcus said.

Sara and I looked at each other, her face mirroring the shock and loss I felt within me. Even though she may have known intellectually that Bonnie's time had come, that she was *dead* dead, she was compelled to connect the dots again in her mind. Now that she had, it was like losing Bonnie all over again. There was no comfort in knowing that she would have died anyway.

Without an alternate version of events in which Bonnie and I continued to be a cherished part of the Classion family, there was nothing to rage at. Uncle Jensen and Aunt Melissa were better off not remembering a daughter they once had than having to spend a lifetime with only her memories and all the what-ifs and could-have-beens her untimely demise would have inundated them with.

A loud knock on the door pierced our thoughts.

We all jumped.

Marcus shot to the ceiling, while I landed on the floor and scurried under the bed, that age-old instinct to hide overcoming me. Only Sara remained against the wall she had been leaning on although I suspect her heart might have given a little lurch. Or maybe not. After all these years of seeing phantoms, she was not easily spooked.

"Come in," she called out.

The door opened and someone walked in. "Lunch is ready. I've been call—" It was Mom's voice. Normal for a moment, but completely trailed off now.

It wasn't hard to guess what may have transpired. The walls of the room had undergone too massive a transformation to escape Mom's notice.

"What's all this?" Mom asked, her voice barely a croak.

"Research, Mom," Sara drawled in that bored, nasal tone teenagers tended to adopt when they didn't want to be badgered with questions they'd rather not answer. "Prepping for my Family History and Lineage course when school reopens."

A snort escaped my mouth and I had to clamp my hand over it. I was willing to bet the rest of my quasi-life that Sara was pulling the wool over Mom's eyes. She was a quick thinker. Hell, yeah!

I crawled noiselessly towards the edge to get a closer look at Mom. She took two steps closer to the bed. All I could see of her was her old, white sneakers, ankle socks peeping out from under her sneakers, and the hem of her light cotton capri pants. It was Mom's signature outfit for the summer. Always ready for an outdoor walk through the fields or the woods, although she spent most of her time indoors, cooking or pottering about the house.

She started walking backwards, making her way towards the door, muttering something about lunch being ready and how Sara should take it a little easy, chill out some, and that it wasn't necessary to be taking on schoolwork before the term even began.

"Don't worry, Mom. This is my way of chilling out. You know that," Sara said, holding the door open for Mom.

Mom sighed. "You work too much."

And then she turned and walked out of the room. Sara closed the door behind her, but not before something bright and shiny blinked and winked at me through the momentarily narrow gap that appeared between the frame and the door before Sara shut it.

I sprang up at the sudden vision, quite forgetting where I was, and bumped my head on the underside of the bed.

"Ow!" I yelled.

"You okay down there?" Sara was on all fours and bending down to peer at me under the bed.

"Yes," I said, crawling out from under the bed, taking care to not invite any more bumps and bruises along the way. At times like these, I wished I had been an untouchable ghost. Mercifully, I kept that thought to myself and didn't express my sentiment aloud. Because as I crawled out, I saw Marcus had been crouching beside the chest of drawers under the window.

"*You* don't need to hide," I said to him.

"Habit," he replied as he straightened himself.

"Neither do you, for that matter," Sara said to me. She stood with her arms folded, watching us with an amused expression on her face.

"Habit." I spread my arms out helplessly.

"For someone who has the gift of invisibility, you two are quite the scaredy-cats." She chuckled. "Back to work now. Chop chop!"

She spun around to take another look at the family tree. Marcus joined her, while I remained seated on the floor beside the bed, rubbing my head where I had bumped it.

The world looked different from this vantage point. The room was larger. Marcus and Sara appeared taller than I knew them to be. They presented quite the contrast, standing beside each other. One was tall and well-built but becoming quite diaphanous as the days passed, I could see now. The other was slim and slender but way more substantial. One was dressed for ruggedness in riding attire. The other was more casual, dressed in a smart pink blouse and black skirt and light pink loafers. Casual chic would have been the word for it.

It was the sight of Sara's loafers that reminded me of what I had seen. Here, in this room, a few moments ago. And there, in my old bedroom, now Sara's room, in the family home downtown, several days ago.

"You need to talk to Mom," I said.

Marcus and Sara turned back to look at me.

"Whatever for?" Sara asked.

"She was in your room a few days ago," I said.

"You mean here?" Sara said.

"No," I shook my head. It was still sore from the bump. "Back at home. The day I brought these boxes from Grandma's and Grandpa's room. She was rummaging through your chest of drawers."

For I knew with utmost certainty, that it was the sole reflective sticker on Mom's left shoe that had glinted in the light as she had walked out of the room.

CHAPTER 22
CONFRONTATION AND COMPREHENSION

Marcus tucked himself under the stairs while I crouched across the landing from him, pressed between a sofa chair and a wall that separated the living room from the kitchen. I kept one ear glued to the wall but that wasn't necessary. Sara's discussion, or, should I say, confrontation, with Mom didn't take long to escalate into a heated argument. They stayed in the kitchen though, Sara having chosen this opportune time, when Mom was cooking, to corner her and demand some answers.

Mom had feigned ignorance at first and when that didn't work, she had turned to denial, all the while stirring a stew on the cooktop that didn't need to be touched. Finally, she covered the dish with a lid and turned to face Sara.

"And how would you come to know, young lady, if I had actually been in your room and looking through your chest of drawers?" Mom asked.

"Aha!" The glee in Sara's voice was undeniable. "So you're no longer denying it then?"

"I was just saying, hypothetically." Mom held her ground,

not at all flustered. "But now you're the one evading my question. Even if something like that had transpired, how would you find out about it?"

Sara was quiet for a moment. Anticipation hung in the hot, humid air, riding on the back of the shrill song of cicadas outside.

"Are you sure you really want to know?" she asked, the defiance and hurt in her voice so chilling it stilled my heart. Even Marcus froze where he was, if such a thing were possible for him.

"Why?" Mom whispered. "What is it?" Dread laced her voice.

Sara dropped the mic. "Becca saw you."

AT THE MENTION of my name, I fell back to the floor with a thud as if the unexpected force of Sara's words had pushed me down. I scrambled back into my earlier squat, half-expecting Mom to come storming out to investigate the source of the sound, to take this perfect distraction I had provided to wriggle out of the corner Sara had pushed her against.

It was the kind of revelation that should have coaxed the truth out of even the most stubborn secret keepers.

But in the heat of the moment, I had forgotten that Mom would have registered the sound of my presence for only an instant and then completely forgotten all about it.

And so it stung when she merely replied, "Becca? Who's Becca? There's no Becca here."

I had half a mind to step out from my hiding place and peer around the wall to get a look at Mom's face if only to ensure her amnesia was authentic. Even after all these years, I hadn't come to grips with the fact that my family had forgotten all about me. It was so easy to forget, this harsh reality of mine.

I heard a click—the sound of the cooktop knob being turned off—and Mom stormed out of the kitchen and straight up the stairs.

"We're leaving tomorrow right after lunch," she hollered on her way up. "Better start packing."

Sara dashed out of the kitchen and came to the bottom of the stairs. She looked up and shouted, "Why won't you talk to me about these things?"

A door slammed in reply.

"You always do this," Sara shouted, defeated, her words failing to reach Mom's ears.

Zelda chose that unfortunate moment to come down the stairs, her mobile phone in one hand and a pair of wireless earphones accessorising her ears. It was only the third or fourth time I had seen her during their stay at the farmhouse this year. She was the spitting image of Sara—that much hadn't changed—but there was a coldness, a certain aloofness to her beauty that made me want to look away and walk out of her life.

Gone was the beautiful golden girl with the golden heart. In her place stood a teenager, just as lost and broken as any other, left with no recourse but to harden herself against the madness that life flung at her.

I now understood the full implication of the curse that Marcus's ancestor had flung our way. Death is hardly ever about the person who's gone. All its effects linger on the ones left behind.

In the same vein, my disappearance, and Bonnie's, and Martha's had slowly been leaching joy and life from the remaining members of the Classion family. Worse still, any knowledge that may have helped them overcome this misfortune was kept from them. Irretrievably so. Leaving no room for recovery. No hope for healing. No recourse from a loss that couldn't be defined. No overcoming a grief that couldn't be explained.

"What's going on?" Zelda asked.

Sara showed her the finger. Zelda shook her head and went back the way she had come, no doubt deciding that her virtual world with access to all three of her boyfriends was a safer haven than this farmhouse of quarrelling ladies.

When Zelda left, Sara plonked herself on the sofa I was hiding behind and lay down, stretching her legs and planting an arm over her eyes. Marcus silently drifted through the kitchen door and disappeared up the creek. I snuck out from where I was hiding and crouched beside Sara, wondering if she wanted me to stay or leave.

Anger and disappointment radiated from her like a heatwave. I ran a light hand over her hair. She did not flinch. But she did not lean towards me either. I peeled myself away from her side and after a moment's thought, in which I debated between staying at home and taking off after Marcus, I opted for the former and went back up to my room, our room.

The investigation room. Where all the secrets of our family lay hidden in plain sight. Names and pictures that had reappeared on the wall after having gone missing for decades. Relationships that had sprung back to life after having been forgotten for several lifetimes. And they had brought with them old hurts and long-forgotten angst, and reopened wounds we had mistakenly thought had healed only to find them still festering under the scars.

Darkness had settled all around us by the time Sara came back to the room. I had stayed there all evening, watching the light outside the south-facing window change, but only imagining the descent of the sun over the horizon. I could have gone to the lavender fields to delight in the splendour of sunset, but I didn't want Sara to come up here and not find me. Nor did I want to behold a sunset alone, so used to her company out in the fields had I grown these past several days.

Tears rolled down my cheeks. The thought that Sara, Zelda, Mom and Dad, and all the others would leave tomorrow crushed me. In just more than a fortnight, I had forgotten the life of solitude I had endured for five years.

I had forgotten how quiet the farmhouse became after summer. Even in the previous years, when the family had not visited, the fields and the gift shop had been abuzz with farmhands bustling about and tourists frolicking in the lavender beauty and calm that was such a delight to their senses. And when the season ended, everyone left, taking all that delight and joy with them, leaving nothing behind for me to hold on to except the hope that another summer would come rolling by.

I was in bed, where I had lain for several hours, feeling sad and lost, when Sara opened the door slowly, stealthily, and crept in and crawled into bed. She reeked of clove and smoke, and I knew she must have been out in the fields by herself.

Resentment gnawed at my insides. I turned towards her and propped myself up on one elbow, the urge to lash out at her already growing stronger inside me. Even in the pale light of the night, I could see her face was swollen and her eyes were red-rimmed and puffed up with grief and rage. Yet again, I bit my tongue and forced my own grief down my throat. By this time, tomorrow, my sister would be gone and once again I'd be alone in this part of the world, reliving these past few days, feeling joy and loss in alternate waves, and finding no one to ride those waves with.

"That didn't go well, did it?" She broke into my reverie.

"Perhaps we were too optimistic," I said. Looking back now, it was easy to see why Mom had exploded the way she did. No one ever wants to admit wrongdoing, no matter how well-intentioned their deed may have been. And how foolish we had been to expect that posing a simple question to her would have elicited just as straightforward an answer.

"But you're sure it was her?"

"Absolutely."

Sara lay staring at the ceiling. I followed her gaze and looked up. The ceiling fan with an ornate light fixture at its centre gawked back at us. No chandelier to twinkle at us like the cluster of a million stars back in our grandparents' room. No fairy lights here like in our room back at the townhome to light up the night.

Something niggled at me. I couldn't stop thinking of the day I had gone back home a few weeks ago when everyone had been here at the farmhouse. Everyone, except Mom, that is. She had taken something from Sara's chest of drawers, I was certain. And something else became apparent too in that instant.

"Sara," I said, turning back to look at her. "What do you think Mom was looking for in your drawers?"

Sara let out a deep breath and squeezed her eyes shut. Tears trickled out of the corner of her eyes and slid down towards her temples. I thought she wouldn't answer but after a long time, she spoke so softly that I had to strain to hear even in the stillness of the night. "A copy of my birth certificate."

"Your birth certificate? What does that have to do with anything?"

I don't think I had ever tried to guess what secret Mom would have wanted to unearth from Sara's dresser. Heck, I hadn't even known until this morning that it had been Mom slinking about in Sara's room that day.

But even if I had tried to conjecture, a certificate stamped by the government attesting to Sara's date and time of birth would never have crossed my mind. What was the secret in it?

"My birth certificate was fake," Sara whispered.

"What do you mean?"

"Precisely that. The piece of paper that Mom and Dad have used everywhere to prove I was born to them on the date and time it claims is fake."

My sister was making no sense. "What is fake about it?"

"Just one tiny thing."

"What?" I said, trying to keep my impatience in check, but Sara was taking too long to tell her story. Something tugged at my gut, an unpleasant sensation, indicating that the world as I knew it was about to collapse. Unravel and crumble into more pieces than it already has. And nothing would be the same ever again. I wanted Sara to speak out, and fast.

"The time," she murmured.

"What about it, Sara honey?" I asked, resisting the urge to shake her and jiggle the words out of her mouth faster than she was letting them out.

"It says I was born at 7:43 in the evening."

"But that's right," I almost screamed, half-mad, half-relieved. "You and Zelda were born in the evening. I remember that because I refused to go to bed until I saw you two. Grandma drove me to the hospital later that night, and I was so excited about getting to stay up so late."

Sara remained quiet and I vowed to keep my mouth shut until she spoke again. I was nervous too and that was making me babble, but I didn't want that to give Sara an excuse to keep her lips sealed. Not when she was this close to telling me what was going on.

Tears were streaming heavily down her cheeks. She sat up, then turned to grab a tissue from the side table and blew into it. She drew her legs close to her chest and wrapped her arms around them, hunching herself up into one large bundle of nerves.

"The time had been altered," she said, staring ahead. "It should have been 7:13."

"That's a difference of half an hour."

"A difference of a lifetime." She buried her face between her knees and began to sob. Her shoulders shook and her body trembled. I rubbed her back, worried she'd fall ill from the tears she was shedding incessantly.

Enlightenment still eluded me. How did it matter that Sara was born half an hour earlier than what her birth certificate claimed? As far as I knew, our family did not put much stock in astrology and was not crazy about drawing up birth charts and natal horoscopes for any of us. I remember becoming obsessed with Linda Goodman's work in my early teens, but not for longer than a season. Did Sara now belong to a different sun sign? Is that what bothered her?

Unable to arrive at a rational explanation for Sara's

outburst, I relented and pleaded with her for an answer. "I don't get it," I said. "Why is it a problem?"

She snapped her head up and looked at me with bloodshot eyes. "Because it makes me the older one," she said and bawled. Her wail splintered the dark of the night as yet another fact I had never questioned in all my life turned on its head and revealed itself to be a lie.

Because this is what Sara was trying to tell me. That she was older than Zelda.

Sara. The child whose life had been cast in the mould of the younger twin. The one who was given the role of the follower, because she was a little too late to arrive in this world. Or so we had all believed. Well, not everybody. Because somebody had known the truth and gone to great lengths to alter it. And the child lived out the consequences of their meddling. Both the twins, actually.

For what would Zelda have become had she not been crowned the older one? The one to look up to? The one to lead? The one to be followed?

What would Sara have become had she not been named the follower? The tag-along?

And then there was the bigger question. Why?

What was to be gained from changing the order in which Sara and Zelda had been born? Who had done this? Had it been Mom? Someone else?

Somewhere in the distance, a fox shrieked. Another responded. I couldn't tell if it was a call of delight or distress. But it explained why no one had come barging into this room yet. Sara had been wailing her heart out, yet not one soul had been roused from slumber or had stepped out of their room into ours to make inquiries. Or perhaps everyone kept their distance because no one wanted to answer the uncomfortable questions Sara was sure to hurl their way.

Countless questions swirled in my head, threatening to drag me down into an emotional whirlpool.

I slipped out of bed and flicked on the light switch. Sara was a mess. "What are you doing?" Her voice was raw and hoarse, worn down by all the sorrow choking her throat.

"Neither of us is getting any sleep tonight," I said with newfound conviction. "Let's get to work. Find out what the bloody hell has been going on in our lives."

She jumped out of bed with more alacrity than I had expected, which gave me hope that no matter what secrets we unearthed, Sara would find a way to carry on and not be dragged under the weight of all that had been done to us, all that had been hidden from us.

Sara posted herself in front of the family tree and continued to scrutinise it for any new clue, any missing link.

I picked up the three boxes of documents one at a time and dumped their contents on the bed once more. Given what Sara had said to me about her time of birth having been modified, I decided to go through the documents this time and put away everything else, including all the photographs and trinkets and memorabilia. They were beautiful to look at, no doubt. More evocative of the past. But over the past few days, I had stared at them long enough that these images were burned in the inside of my eyes and I could recall every little detail with my eyes closed.

There were very few documents to peruse.

Zelda's and Sara's papers were unlikely to be here, I realised. Mom and Dad would have kept the originals in the safe in their bedroom at the townhome and copies in the family locker at the bank. Mine would have been there too for as long as I had been a tangible part of their lives. Not anymore.

I didn't know what I was looking for, so I examined everything thoroughly. There were four file folders in all.

I had already perused them the day I had brought them to the farmhouse. It had been the day I had found a record of Martha's birth. Proof of her existence in this world, in our lives.

My grandparents had been meticulous record keepers, phantom disappearances notwithstanding. The files were labelled chronologically, each spanning up to two decades.

The latest folder, the only one bearing documents from the twenty-first century, was the thinnest of them all. The admin task must have proven too difficult for my grandparents to keep up with in their old age, I reckoned, and Dad and Uncle Jensen may have shouldered much of that responsibility.

It seemed like a good idea to begin right at the beginning. Chronology would lend some semblance of order to the chaos that seemed to rule our lives now.

Handwritten records of my grandparents' births. Long, sloping lines and curves spelling out their names and every detail of their births. At 6 lbs, 5 ounces, Grandma had been a small baby. Even in old age, she had been of slight stature, appearing even more diminutive against Grandpa's domineering height when he could still walk. When Grandpa was banished to a wheelchair, he still came almost up to Grandma's shoulders.

A soft, scratching sound made me look up. Sara was scribbling furiously on the wall. Guilt pricked me and I made a concerted effort to not lose myself to the temptation of reimagining and romanticising the past.

The first two folders revealed nothing of interest. The third folder was the one in which I had come across Martha's birth record. I looked through it once more but nothing new had materialised in here.

I picked up the fourth folder, already feeling hopeless. There were only a handful of papers tucked in here. Copies of Zelda's and Sara's birth certificates. A welcome surprise. Perhaps my grandparents had insisted on holding on to extra copies, just in case. I looked at the papers more closely now. Yes. Sara's certificate clearly stated she had been born at 7:13 PM while Zelda's recorded her time of birth as 7:31 PM. Eighteen minutes too late.

In my hands, the two documents were almost identical, barring the names of my sisters and their times of birth. I held Sara's record to the light above to see if the alteration was still discernible. The '1' was clear. There was no way it could be mistaken for a '4' anymore. The truth had planted itself back clearly on the page.

I held Zelda's record to the light to see if it had secrets to reveal too. It did. The paper, just as flimsy as Sara's, had some additional print on it. It appeared vague, the letters were not clearly formed. And there was something odd about its shape. It was not a perfect rectangle. As if it had been stretched out along the top right corner. Grown a fox ear or something.

Turned out it was another sheet of paper attached to it. I held on to the extended corner and tried to peel away the sheet that appeared stuck to the back of Zelda's record.

'Record of Birth', it said in beautiful calligraphy at the top.

To whomsoever it may concern, it said in a handwriting font just below the heading.

This is to certify that Martha Y. Classion gave birth to a baby girl, Rebecca Classion, 8 pounds and 5 ounces in weight, 19.5 inches in height, at 0649 hours on the twenty-first day of the seventh month of the year two thousand and one.

My heart exploded in my chest. Blood pounded in my ears. My eyes brimmed with tears and the words on the paper dissolved into a blur.

July 21, 2001.

That was my date of birth.

Rebecca Classion.

That was me.

"Sara," I cried out weakly as the paper slipped from my hand.

Through tear-filled eyes, I saw my sister spin around and run to me. All colour had drained from her face, as if she had read my thoughts, heard my anguish, and I didn't have to voice it out loud. Impossible. But a small mercy I was grateful for in that moment.

I'd have said she looked white as a ghost but both of us knew, and by now you do too, that that was not what ghosts looked like. Devoid of colour. No. Devoid of substance, yes, but not devoid of colour.

"Becca," she called out, gripping my arms so tight it made me wince. "Becca!" She shook me. In my stupor, her voice sounded distant and muffled. Sound waves swam through a muck of secrets and revelations that fouled the air between the two of us.

Her eyes were wide, as if the world she had known,

already fractured and cleaved countless times, had splintered once again.

And when we spoke, it was at the same time. Each of us spilling the discovery we had made.

"Martha was my mom," I whimpered.

"Mom was an Ahlgren," Sara shouted.

CHAPTER 23
IMPOSSIBLE TRUTHS

We both stared at each other, stunned into silence. Whoever said that the truth sets you free, must have known only one side of the story. Or, more likely, they must have merely glossed over the finer details, reluctant to reveal all the pain and anguish that precedes the illusory freedom so sought after.

Nevertheless, as shocking as it was, Sara's announcement distracted me from the improbability of my own finding. Mom was an Ahlgren. Mom was an Ahlgren? Mom? Could I even call her that anymore? An Ahlgren in our family.

"How did you find out?" I asked. My voice sounded feeble to my own ears, so I cleared my throat and repeated myself, louder this time. "How did you find out?"

Sara was looking at me curiously. No doubt she had heard my declaration too. She bent down and picked up the paper that had slipped from my fingers and fallen to the side of the bed. I watched her as she read it, as comprehension stretched her features, pulled her eyes wide open, forced her mouth into a wide O, and pushed tears out of her green eyes. She ran a hand through her hair, her beautiful golden locks, and clutched them tight, momentarily tugging at her scalp, ensuring the paper in her hand and the words on it were as real as the pain her fingers were transferring through her locks and inflicting on her scalp.

She looked up at me, unable to compose herself. She was trying hard though, I could see. But her tears fell and she whimpered, "This is not true. It cannot be. It cannot be." As if saying something out loud over and over again would make it true.

And why not? We become the stories we tell ourselves repeatedly. And before a mere piece of paper had appeared out of the ether and declared otherwise, I had been my parents' daughter, Zelda had been the older twin, and Sara had been the youngest among us. Martha had not existed in our lives, not in any way that mattered. Bonnie was gone, as if she too had never come into our lives.

"How do you know this refers to you?" Sara was shouting in my face. Her words were still distant, as if coming from another room. Another planet. Words having lost their momentum long before they fell on my ears. Like starlight. Already decades older than they used to be before we could discern them.

Sara was trying to shake me, but her grip faltered. "You're fading," she said, looking at her hands as if they had somehow failed her.

I looked down at myself. If something about me had changed, it wasn't evident to me. I put a hand out to touch Sara, but nothing came into my grasp. She reached out again but her fingers just passed through me as if I didn't exist. All I felt was a mere disturbance of air, a breath, a ripple in my being. Nothing significant. Nothing substantial.

"Am I dying?" I asked her. "Like *really* dying this time?"

Sara shook her head, whether in denial or to answer me in the negative, I couldn't tell. She tried to speak but tears smothered her words. Nothing she said was intelligible.

Perhaps, this was the truth I needed to learn before truly giving up the ghost. That I was not my mother's daughter.

I didn't know how to feel about that. Joy? That I had been cared for by the very family into which I had been born? Grief? That my mother had been erased from existence so completely that even her daughter had held no memory of her? Anger? That no one had told me about it? But how could they have? They too had forgotten it all, hadn't they?

When I thought about it and allowed myself to feel it, the emotion that rose to the surface with immense force was fear. Terror. I had been scared of so many things. Above all, of being disowned. But I had already been disowned, I remembered. I had already been forgotten. What was there to fear now?

Sara's voice brought me back to her presence. "You're very faint but you're not gone yet," she sobbed.

Exhaustion overwhelmed me. I leaned back against the pillows and closed my eyes.

"Stay with me," Sara said.

I smiled. Silly girl, I thought. I was already gone in every way that mattered.

Outside, a robin trilled. Demanding that the world wake up and hear its sweet song.

Something fluttered against my cheeks. I opened my eyes.

It took a great deal of effort. Sara was trying to slap me on the cheek, the way one does to keep a dying person conscious. My sister had already forgotten I was nothing more than a ghost, even in this state of quasi-existence. It was a truth I had denied too for as long as I could, until Sara had come, her ability to see me serving as some kind of a lifeline. A reason to exist.

And now, there was nothing more to hold on to.

So I let go.

CHAPTER 24
FINAL FAREWELL

When I came to, I found myself still lying on the same bed in the same room. It was late morning; I could tell from the way a sliver of sunshine spilled into the room and illuminated the family tree on the wall opposite the bed.

Marcus sat at the foot of the bed. When he saw me stir, he drifted noiselessly out of the room, through the door, and came back moments later.

The door swung open behind him. Sara ran into the room, her eyes searching, finding relief at the sight of me. I was still tethered to this realm then. Not yet completely gone. Not *dead* dead yet.

I sat up, invigorated at the sight of my sister. That was when I saw Mom. She was in the room, standing behind Marcus. She now walked around him and stood by the side of the bed. Behind her, Marcus drifted towards the window and perched himself atop the chest of drawers there. Mom's gaze followed his movement. When he had settled, she turned to look at me. She could *see* me.

"Mom?" I whispered. Heart in mouth. Hoping against hope. So many impossible things had happened. Why not one more?

"Becca," she whispered, and her face crumpled into tears. She sat on the bed and reached out a hand to touch my face, but it slipped through me, and all I caught was a whiff of her lavender perfume.

But she could see me, and my heart leapt with joy, even though her shoulders heaved with sobs and anguish wrecked her soul.

"You can see me?!" A question. Also, a realisation.

She nodded and glanced at Sara. Something passed between them. An understanding. They must have had a long conversation in the time I had spent asleep, having slipped away from this world a bit more. But I had come back here, which meant there were truths that were yet to be clarified to me. But there was no denying it. My time had come. My story was inching towards its conclusion.

"Sara inherited her gift of sight," Mom said.

"From you?"

"Yes."

Now that Mom mentioned it, it was so obvious. It was something we had never thought of investigating. The source of Sara's abilities.

"Why did you deny it then?"

Mom shrugged. "You've seen for yourself," she said. "It's not easy living with something like this."

"It's even harder having to live with something like this all by yourself." My voice grew louder. "You could have helped her cope with it."

Mom sighed. She had probably placated Sara already on all

these fronts, but these were not wounds that could be healed in a single conversation. Sara and Mom were going to have to cover the same grounds over and over again in the coming weeks and months. Even years.

"Becca, honey," she said, finally. "There are many things I should have done differently. That's the trouble with hindsight. It heaps blame on us but rarely shines a light on the path ahead. It doesn't show us which way to go."

Mom's explanation made sense, but I also felt as if she were trying to wriggle out of this easily. She needed to shoulder the blame. I was angry and I wanted to hold someone responsible for it. I wanted someone else to pay the price for it. And right now, Mom was the perfect target. The one person who could have saved us a lot of trouble and heartache but didn't.

I pouted and sulked, determined to not conceal all that I felt right then. Anger. Sorrow. Disappointment.

"So where are we supposed to go from here?" I asked.

"I believe you need the truth to set you free," she said. "You and Marcus," she added, throwing him a glance over her shoulder.

"I already know it," I barked. "You're not my Mom. Martha was."

Pain exploded on Mom's face, and it gave me immense satisfaction to see that. There was a certain joy in being able to hurt someone who had caused you grievous harm. But as satisfying as it was, it was also fleeting. It didn't make me feel good about myself. Instead, I was instantly filled with self-loathing and guilt. Mom had raised me as her own daughter, never having treated me any differently than Zelda and Sara.

"Martha gave birth to you, yes." Her voice was stern. "But I raised you. And you are my daughter, whether you like it or not."

Her soft face appeared drawn. Her eyes were bloodshot. She must have spent a sleepless night too, like Sara and I. Haunted by ghosts, both real and of her own making.

"And are you an Ahlgren?" I asked.

Marcus slipped from the top of the dresser where he had been sitting. "You are an Ahlgren?" His eyes had grown twice their size in astonishment.

"Yes," Sara piped up, before Mom could answer. "You've got to see this." She made her way to the wall and Mom shifted a little on the bed, so I had a better view.

"I spent hours staring at the tree," Sara began, "and I thought maybe I ought to look into the past. Not of those who were Classions by birth. But of others who became part of our family by marriage or adoption or any other reason."

"And?" Marcus and I leaned forwards to get a better look.

"Grandma, Aunt Melissa, and Mom were the ones I began with." Sara was clearly enjoying this moment of limelight when everybody's attention was only on her. "I began with their maiden names. Wrote them out in full. Wrote out the initials. And then I saw it."

She stood to the side and pointed to a particular patch on the wall where she had written Mom's name and scratched it out and written it down in myriad ways.

Curious, I slipped out of bed and floated towards her. It was only when I was halfway through the room did I notice that I wasn't walking. My gait was no longer a shuffling of one foot in front of the other. I was floating a few inches above the ground.

"Whoa," I said.

That moment of realisation turned out to be my undoing. When I saw myself adrift and couldn't quite believe it, I fell to the ground in a heap. Marcus swooped down towards me and helped me back on my feet and then into mid-air again, all the while grinning in the most ungentlemanly way. "Pardon me," he said, "but you were a natural until you realised it. Just trust yourself. You don't have to think too much about it."

Easier said than done. He let go of me and I found myself leaning towards him, somehow reaching out for support as he backed away, and in the process, I rendered myself horizontal. Like a lady levitating under a magician's nose, gleefully waiting for her body to be sliced into three parts. Only, not quite as elegant.

I flailed and thrashed my limbs about, fighting for purchase, but my efforts only caused me to drift further up towards the ceiling.

"Relax," Marcus called out as he floated up and drew level. I looked down. Huge, uncontrollable grins were splashed across Mom's and Sara's upturned faces. Everyone was having a blast at my expense. Oh, well! At least something hilarious came out of this tragedy that had been unfolding in our lives for generations.

"How exactly?" I asked Marcus.

"Don't think about it."

But all I could think about was getting myself to the ground and learning about how Sara had stumbled upon the one discovery that had given us our big break in this investigation. This was her Poirot moment, and I didn't want to steal her thunder.

I craned my neck to look at the wall, and without much intervention on my part, my body, or whatever I could call this wraithlike form of mine, righted itself. Like a feather, I drifted down to the ground and turned into an upright position.

The less I thought about my movement and the more I focussed on Sara and the family tree on our wall, the wall of secrets, the more effortless it became. Sometimes it was so much easier to do something for another than for oneself.

There was an urge to let out a breath. A sigh. But no air escaped my lungs. There was no breath in me. That vital, life-sustaining element was gone.

"You did it," Sara clapped and jumped in glee. "Okay, before you float away again, let me show you how I solved that mystery."

"Mom's maiden name," I said to indicate I had been paying attention.

Sara beamed. "Heather Rainier Lange."

"H. R. L.?"

"Try H. R. Lange."

"Her signature?" The one that Sara had so expertly rendered on the wall with practised ease.

And there it was. The letters rearranged themselves to present *Ahlgren*.

Sara shone with pride. I turned back to look at Mom. She nodded. Tears streamed down her cheeks and she wiped them away, only to make room for more to follow. Marcus kept looking at each of us, one at a time, trying to discern an explanation. He kept working his jaw, as though he were chewing and attempting to digest this piece of information but found it to be a mighty struggle.

I shrugged my shoulders and shook my head. I knew only as much as Sara had revealed now. Marcus looked at her, but she pointed towards Mom too. We all waited for Mom to speak up, and I found myself growing impatient with the time it was taking her to collect herself and start uttering the words that would shed light on everything.

"My great grandfather had two sisters," Marcus said. "We never knew what became of them."

Mom finally spoke. "Yes. The older sister was my great grandmother."

Marcus's eyes nearly popped out of his head. It was quite comical to witness such expression in someone who was otherwise pretty good at maintaining a poker face. Today's truths were causing Marcus to unravel too, I realised.

"So you're my third cousin?" he asked, his voice strangely shrill.

"Yes," Mom said.

"Are there others too? Where did you grow up? What about your parents? Are they still alive? Tell me ... tell me everything. And how did you marry into the Classion family?" Questions poured out of him in a torrent. And then he turned to me, hesitated for a moment, then looked to Sara and beamed. "We're related. You and I. You're an Ahlgren too!"

I understood his hesitation a moment ago. I was born to Martha, not to Mom, and that meant there was no Ahlgren blood flowing through my veins. And for the first time I wondered who my father was. If not Dad, then who was my father?

"We're not the first to try and break our ancestor's curse," Mom began. "Our great grandparents thought that by moving away from this land, by separating themselves from each other, maybe, just maybe, a line of Ahlgrens would emerge free from the curse. But no such luck." She shook her head.

"Our ancestor's curse meant that just as the Classions would never remember, the Ahlgrens would never forget."

"Were there Classions in your part of the world too?"

"No," Mom said. "So many of them had been eradicated we … you all … are the only remaining ones."

"Marrying a Classion did not make you one?" I asked.

"In name only. Ahlgren blood still courses through my veins. Marriage could hardly change that."

"Mom," I said. "Is that why I too remained a Classion? Who was my father?" I clenched my fists. There was no sensation, no feeling of grip that could help me contain the conflicting emotions I felt. Wanting to know. And not wanting new facts to completely erase what I had believed until last night, that Mom and Dad were my parents.

Mom wrung her hands for a few moments, then she met my gaze and said, "Martha never married. We never found out who your biological father was."

An illegitimate child. That was who I was. Born to a teenage mother. No older than I had been when Marcus had asked me to walk away with him. No older than Sara was now. And Zelda too.

If she hadn't been bound by the curse and doomed to die, would my mother have still wanted to keep me? A strange laugh escaped my lips. It sounded bitter to me.

"Now don't go labelling yourself based on the laws of the government and the rules of society," Mom said, reading my thoughts. "My ancestor's spell transcended all these manmade definitions and boundaries. Even if Martha had married, you'd have remained a firstborn Classion, and an Ahlgren would have come for you sooner or later. I'm only glad your fate unfolded when you were still part of our family. Those fifteen years with you were priceless, especially as I knew what lay in store for you."

Mom spoke with so much earnestness and I knew she was telling the truth, but I had to make an effort to believe everything she said. Because the truth was so simple. Everyone had been bound by a curse. There was no one to blame. No one to point fingers at.

Well, the Ahlgren matron who had hurled the curse in a moment of insanity certainly deserved to shoulder much of the blame. But she had been bereaved too. Grief had driven her out of her mind.

Not having someone to blame, someone to accuse, someone to punish for all the wrongs that had come to pass, left me a little deflated.

"How did you come to marry Dad?" Sara asked.

"I better narrate this in order," Mom said. "After my great grandmother moved away from here, she did not speak of the Ahlgren curse at first, thinking that would diminish its hold on us somehow. But as she lay on her deathbed, she unburdened herself to her son, my grandfather. He was a gentle soul. The possibility that he would be compelled to ruin a Classion's life tormented him for the rest of his life. He drank himself to death."

Here she paused. To catch a breath. To indulge in reminiscence. Or perhaps, stunned by the realisation that a story told aloud to a rapt audience sounds vastly different than when we keep telling it to ourselves in our heads.

"That was another thing the Ahlgren men were supposedly known for," Marcus said. "For the drunken brawls they indulged in. But the village turned a blind eye to the din and clamour they caused. Blamed it on the grief brought about by their loss."

"Were you too a victim of that misfortune?" Mom asked.

"I worked in a distillery," Marcus smirked. "It ruined my ability to appreciate a good drink once and for all."

Mom nodded. "I suppose my grandfather drank to forget but that's the one thing we Ahlgrens can never do. We can never forget. Whereas my great-grandmother tried her hardest to keep the whole thing under wraps, my grandfather ranted and raved about the curse, and it became the only thing he ever talked about. It was all a jumble though. He never made much sense. And we didn't take him seriously. But when he died, I saw his spirit. What he had spent a life-time running away from, he was forced to encounter in death."

"Did he come for Martha?" I asked.

"Yes," Mom said.

"What about your father? And his siblings?" Marcus asked.

"My father and his brother are still alive," Mom said, "which is likely why the burden of carrying out the curse fell on you this time."

"But how did you end up marrying a Classion?" Sara asked.

Mom sighed. "I tempted fate," she said. "I moved back here to study." She drew air quotes as she said that. "Well, on the pretext of pursuing higher studies. I wanted to know if all the stories my grandfather had revealed about our family in his drunken state were indeed true. Guess I was curious. And I wanted to meet a Classion. It's one thing to harbour animosity against a family you've never met. Classion was just a name, an idea, an abstract notion in my mind. But it's quite impossible to get to know a Classion in flesh and blood and continue to hate them, especially after finding out they are just as human as I am."

Yet another piece of the puzzle clicked into place. When we were younger, our favourite bedtime story had been the one that Mom told of how she met Dad. Her version of the events was that she had fallen head over heels in love with Dad at first sight and had walked straight up to him and asked him out on a date. "If you want something, reach out for it," had been the moral of the story she had wanted to impart to us. No waiting for Prince or Princess Charming to come and whisk you away.

"You didn't marry Dad for love then?" Sara whispered.

Mom's lips trembled. "When I first saw him, when I was first attracted to him, I had no idea who he was. When I found out he was Hugo Classion, it only made me all the more determined to stay by his side. I changed my last name. Never revealed to him I was, still am, an Ahlgren. I thought if the two families came together in marriage, it would undo the spell somehow. Because I was convinced that as much as my ancestor had wanted to hurt the Classion family, she wouldn't have wanted an Ahlgren to suffer the loss of yet another of their own."

Dust motes rose and twirled in the beams of light that the afternoon sun poured generously through the window. We had all been held in the trance of revelation for so long that we hadn't moved. And we hadn't realised how still we had all become.

Marcus, still atop the chest of drawers. Mom, sitting on the edge of the bed. Sara and I between her and the wall bearing the family tree. Sara's feet planted firmly on the ground like the trunk of a tree reaching into the depths of the soil it had sprung from, holding on for strength and stability.

Mine hovering a couple of inches above the floor. Poised for flight. The connection between me and this world severed in some irreversible way.

"I couldn't save you," Mom said to me. "I tried to, but I couldn't."

Because I had no Ahglren blood in me to save me from the fate that lay in store for all firstborn Classions. I didn't hold any grudge against Mom for that. How could I?

"When did Martha ... my mom ... die?" I asked.

"She was taken the night you were born," Mom replied. "Right here. In this very house. In this very room. My grand-father's spirit came for her."

I looked around, as if I'd be able to spot my birth mother's ghost lurking in a corner somewhere, tucked away like a shadow I'd have never thought to give a second glance.

My form throbbed with the weighty sensation of grief. It was just as heavy when I had been fully alive. Even in my quasi-life, it had been the heaviness of all these feelings and sensations that had either weighed me down or propelled me into action. So far, being dead didn't feel all that different from being alive, except for my newfound ability to float and drift, and a greater awareness of my feelings and emotions as weighted blocks, tying me down to this world like gravity.

"The next morning, the story of our lives had changed," Mom continued. "Your grandparents woke up to the unex-pected cries of an infant they had no recollection of expecting in the family. They took you to be an abandoned child, and they took you in. A few years later, when Hugo and I married, we adopted you. You became our firstborn. Martha was utterly and completely forgotten."

"But you remembered."

"I've never forgotten."

"Were you trying to save Sara when you altered her time of birth?" I asked.

Mom glanced at Sara and I turned back to look at my sister. Her face was devoid of expression. I reckoned she had already gone over the details with Mom and the story was being retold for my benefit.

Sara tucked her hand in a pocket I had no idea had been stitched into her skirt and drew out a packet of cigarettes and a lighter. I turned around to look at Mom so swiftly that I thought my head would fly off. Mom simply shook her head and said, "We all have our ways of coping with pain. And Sara has seen the worst of it."

Sara smirked as if Mom's approval, or rather her lack of disapproval, made no difference. She lit up her cigarette and went to sit beside Marcus atop the chest of drawers.

"I was just trying everything I could think of to keep you three safe," Mom said, drawing the conversation back to the thread of the story that began when the twins were born. "I wondered if switching their times of birth would confuse the forces that be. Cause an Ahlgren to make a mistake. Take the wrong soul. A blunder that would undo the spell once and for all."

"It was a blunder, alright," Sara hissed. "In more ways than one." Smoke mingled with her words and made them fluffy. Less potent, somehow.

"Will they be safe?" I asked Mom, ignoring Sara's snide remark. "Zelda and Sara?"

"As long as they stay away from each other, I suppose," Mom said.

"Ha ha! Very funny," Sara mocked.

I wondered if that was how my relationship with Mom would have devolved had I spent more of my teenage years with her. Being guided, scolded, praised, admonished. Being parented. Being loved and fretted about.

On my part, disobeying and rebelling. Longing for an escape. For freedom. A life of my own. Not like the one I got too soon, the one that cost me everything I once knew and held dear. But like the ones Zelda and Sara will experience, if they can manage to spend the next few years without causing each other much hurt or damage.

I drifted towards Mom and tried to sit on the bed, though it didn't feel as if it was strong enough to keep me propped up. I was in eternal danger of slipping through and away, far away.

Mom was spent, I could tell. The dark circles under her eyes showed clearly, like the dark side of the moon made more evident by the bright sliver of it. The corners of her mouth were turned down. All the effort of plastering a smile on her face, when the world around her was only a moment away from crumbling, had come to nought.

"How did you spend all these years bearing this burden alone?" I asked Mom. "Knowing what you knew? A secret that was only yours to keep?"

She smiled at me. "You know the answer to that," she said.

I didn't catch her drift.

"We're only the stories we tell about ourselves, Becca honey," she said. "I told myself I was on a grand adventure to set right a grave mistake. A journey to protect future generations from the misguided wrath of my ancestor. That helped. Even if not always. But I wasn't alone. Not always. When Martha was taken away, I spoke with her, much the way we're having this conversation right now. She trusted I'd look after you well."

Mom involuntarily put a hand out to touch my cheek, but it slipped through my form. She drew back, sad but understanding. A feather touch was all I felt, and I tried to cling to that sensation. In vain.

"You did," I said.

"And your Grandma too couldn't depart until she had learnt the truth of what had happened to her oldest offspring."

"I saw that," Sara said. "I saw Grandma's ghost approaching you, but I didn't know you could see her too."

"You did the best thing," Mom said. "Spirits can be needy, sometimes. They're not always quite like the people we knew them to be. It's best to leave them be."

"You too did your best, Mom," I said.

Tears ran down her cheeks. "It never felt enough," she said.

The sadness in her voice caused something in me to shift. A huge weight that suddenly dissolved in her tears. The urge to placate her grew intense as if my salvation hinged on it. "I never once wanted a different life than the one I had with you," I said, and that was the instant I knew I meant it with all my heart. The relief in Mom's eyes brought the words gushing out of my mouth. "The one time I was really mad at you was the last time we all had a spat on the landing right outside this room. The last time we spoke. Before I was wrenched out of your lives."

Mom smiled through her tears, and it was a smile of relief

and of joy, of sadness and longing, of acceptance and surrender.

Marcus peeled himself away from the chest of drawers and came to stand in front of Mom, holding his hat to his chest. "My time has come," he said. Mom stood up. They were of the same height. Facing each other, they looked like siblings. A brother and a sister. Cousins who should have grown up alongside, trading childhood memories as adults instead of having to unravel family secrets and confront their losses in these few precious moments that were left.

"This is what you'd been waiting for," Mom said. "The truth."

"And a release. Thanks to you, I no longer feel the burden of having to claw yet another Classion out of your lives. Remember me, sister," he said.

Then he turned to me. "I'm sorry," he said.

"Thank you," I whispered.

He turned around to bid farewell to Sara, who was already on her fifth cigarette. She had lined up the cigarette stubs beside her on the dresser. I couldn't tell what she had ground them into to put them out. "Don't burn this place down, dare-devil niece," Marcus winked at her.

"Or maybe I should," Sara said, waving her cigarette around in the air. "Good riddance to bad rubbish." But she grinned after saying that and everyone tittered. She gave Marcus a salute. As if that were the cue he was waiting for, Marcus disappeared in a swirl of smoke. And all that remained were me and my mother and my sister, the smoke from her cigarette more real than the cloud into which Marcus had disappeared.

"Where's everyone else?" I asked.

Marcus's departure brought me back to the reality of the present moment. The four of us had been in this room all day, and not once had we been interrupted. It was evening already. And I wasn't sure why I was still drifting about.

Contrary to what you may believe, the ability to hover and drift isn't a particularly pleasurable sensation. Not at first, at least. Not after a couple of decades of keeping my feet planted firmly on the ground, for the most part that is. Drifting with no destination in mind was just as unsettling as being lost.

"Back in the city," Mom said.

"We'd have left too had you not almost *died* died," Sara said.

The memory of a twin discovery came back to me. Finding out Mom was an Ahlgren. Finding out Mom was not my mother. The truths that had released me from life. Well, almost.

"I wonder where Marcus went," I said.

"I miss him too," Sara said. "Do you think you'll meet the others?"

So many questions rolled into that single one. Where do the souls of the departed go? Will I meet Bonnie? And my mother, Martha? Will I see Marcus again? The Ahlgren matriarch who brought about so much misery to her heirs? All the other Classions and Ahlgrens whose fates were so deeply intertwined with each other's that it only made sense that the two families had united in both the worldly and otherworldly realms?

"Guess I won't live to tell that tale." I was secretly pleased with my own wit, but it only earned me a smirk from Sara.

"Don't come to haunt me," she said, pointing the burning end of her cigarette at me.

"Great idea, Sara! Now I can't not act on it." I giggled.

But inwardly, I felt hollow with all this idle banter. None of us knew what to say to each other. This occasion should have felt significant. This moment of farewell. It seemed as if we were about to bid each other 'Good night' after having spent a long day at work together. Maybe, that's what was needed. Nothing momentous. Nothing heavy. A light-hearted departure. A happy ending. And then it came to me, what I was waiting for.

"I'm about to leave too," I said, rather delighted at having something definitive to look forward to rather than a vague 'what next' to wade my way through.

"You sense it?" Mom stiffened.

"I think so," I said to her. Something tugged at me, and I glided through the door and out of the room. I spun around, even as unseen forces grabbed me as if with imperceptible hands and blew me through the landing to the top of the stairs. I was given a pause, barely enough to see Mom and Sara open the door to the room and run out after me.

"I love you so much," I yelled and continued my journey down the grand staircase and out through the kitchen door, past the creek, around the house until finally I was in the lavender fields.

The sun was slipping behind the horizon, faster than I had ever seen. Sunlight-laced clouds gleamed in the skies, promising the presence of faraway lands, ones that we couldn't see from here but ones that surely existed, ones that we could get closer to if only we sought to put one step in front of another and another and another.

This was what my spirit had been waiting for. One last sunset to behold.

Except, I forgot I wasn't walking anymore. I drifted upwards, chasing the sun in my own way, seeing more and more of the ball of orange, having burnt itself out for the day, from up here than I could possibly have from the fields below where Mom and Sara stood, looking up at me. Mom waved. She reminded me of Zelda as a child waving to every plane or car or stranger that passed her by. Sara held herself still, moving only her arm to bring her cigarette—was it the tenth of that afternoon, I had lost count—to her lips and away. She sent smoke rings my way. Little doughnuts that broke up and dispersed in the aether before they could come anywhere close to me. But I appreciated the gesture.

I waved back to them.

At least, that's what I tried to do.

And I hoped they noticed. For I couldn't even see my own hand in front of my face.

And that was how I knew I was truly gone.

~ THE END ~

ENJOYED ERASED FROM EXISTENCE?

Thank you for reading Erased from Existence!

If you loved the book, I hope you will consider writing a short review—even a simple line or two—on the site where you bought the book.

Publishing is still driven by word of mouth, and when you leave a review it helps other readers decide this is a book worth reading. Thank you for your help in spreading the word.

You can also sign up to my monthly newsletter to read a bonus scene, titled '*Sara's Ruminations*'.

https://thedreampedlar.com/fiction-saras-ruminations/

When you sign up, you will also receive access to additional works of fiction available exclusively to subscribers.

AUTHOR'S NOTE

Dear Reader,

Thank you for finding me here at last, after the end of a story I hope you loved reading.

Over on my website, I have often written about how my writing journey is an act of homecoming. It is akin to a pilgrimage. Every step I take on this journey reveals something to me about myself, my hopes and my fears, my desires and my worries.

Erased from Existence is my second full-length novel following *Dying Wishes*, but the writing and publishing processes of the two books bear little resemblance to each other.

Dying Wishes took me more than two years to write, but once I had penned the last line, I wasted no time in getting the manuscript edited and the book cover designed, and it was published only a couple of months later.

In contrast, *Erased from Existence* took me a few months to write—it is also a much shorter novel than *Dying Wishes* is— but at the time of my writing this missive, I see that I had finished my first draft of the work more than nine months ago.

If you're familiar with my writings, you may have noticed that *Erased from Existence* is very different from my other works thus far.

It is a mystery. There is family history involved. It is set in the countryside. I found myself on unfamiliar ground in several ways. Yet, somehow, that did not hamper my writing of it. In fact, treading uncharted waters added to the excitement of the writing process.

The writing proved so enjoyable, especially in the wake of the lull that the completion of *Dying Wishes* had left, that I simply went on to write other works, several of which I intend to publish in the coming months. *A Benevolent Goddess* was one among them.

And so it was that after *Erased from Existence* came into being on the page, there followed a long hiatus before I could do the necessary work to cast the story into the form of this book you now hold in your hands.

I hope you enjoyed reading the book and learning a little about how it came into being. We've come together so far, and I hope you would like to stay connected with me.

I send out a monthly newsletter on the last Sunday of every month. Subscription is free. When you sign up, you will gain exclusive access to a bonus scene from *Erased from Existence* as well as a bunch of other short fiction available only to subscribers.

You will be the first to hear of my forthcoming works. I will also include updates on my writing life, book recommendations, and occasional surprises.

Thank you for staying with me this far. If you choose to

accompany me further on this journey, I promise you a magical ride.

Delightful dreams and wondrous whimsies. Impossible illusions and fleeting fantasies.

Straight from The Dream Pedlar's emporium into your mailbox!

Climb aboard at https://thedreampedlar.com/newsletter!

~ Anitha Krishnan
Burlington, Ontario
17 July 2022

MORE BOOKS BY ANITHA KRISHNAN

https://thedreampedlar.com/books/

Dying Wishes

A contemporary fantasy novel weaving Hindu mythology and South Indian folklore into a quest for belonging across different worlds — the World of Mortals and the World of Gods, India and Canada, the past and the present, the world outside and the one within.

A Benevolent Goddess

A story of a goddess who is punished for her desire to help human beings but is unable to find salvation by any other means.

In Search of Leo

A fantasy tale exploring the gamut of emotions that loss and grief can stir.

Hello, Dreamer! Poems & Dreams

An eclectic collection of 100 short poems encompassing musings on the universe and its mysteries, nature and human life, my secret longings and fears, love and heartbreak, the sun and the moon, the stars and the seas, light and shadow, and joy and nostalgia.

About the Author

Anitha Krishnan is a speculative fiction author and an award-winning poet. She has lived in and left pieces of her heart in many places across the world including Singapore, Australia, Canada, and most of all in her beloved birthplace, India. She presently lives in Burlington, Ontario with her husband and their cherished child.

Find more books and her blog on the writing life at
https://thedreampedlar.com.

Sign up to her monthly newsletter at
https://thedreampedlar.com/newsletter
to receive heartfelt musings, exclusive updates, book recommendations, free fiction, and more!

facebook.com/DreamPedlar